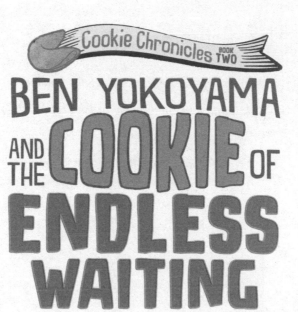

Cookie Chronicles BOOK TWO

BEN YOKOYAMA

AND THE COOKIE OF

THE ENDLESS WAITING

THE COOKIE CHRONICLES

BEN YOKOYAMA
AND THE COOKIE OF
ENDLESS WAITING

BY MATTHEW SWANSON
& ROBBI BEHR

A YEARLING BOOK

Text copyright © 2021 by Matthew Swanson
Cover art and interior illustrations copyright © 2021 by Robbi Behr

All rights reserved. Published in the United States by Yearling, an imprint of Random House Children's Books, a division of Penguin Random House LLC, New York. Originally published in hardcover in the United States by Alfred A. Knopf, an imprint of Random House Children's Books, a division of Penguin Random House LLC, New York, in 2021.

Yearling and the jumping horse design are registered trademarks of Penguin Random House LLC.

Visit us on the Web! rhcbooks.com

Educators and librarians, for a variety of teaching tools, visit us at RHTeachersLibrarians.com

Library of Congress Cataloging-in-Publication Data is available upon request.
ISBN 978-0-593-30276-7 (trade) — ISBN 978-0-593-12687-5 (lib. bdg.) —
ISBN 978-0-593-12688-2 (ebook) — ISBN 978-0-593-12686-8 (paperback)

Printed in the United States of America
10 9 8 7 6 5 4 3 2 1
First Yearling Edition 2022

To Stella, Gunther,
Eddie, and Rafe,
the very best old friends
we could have asked for

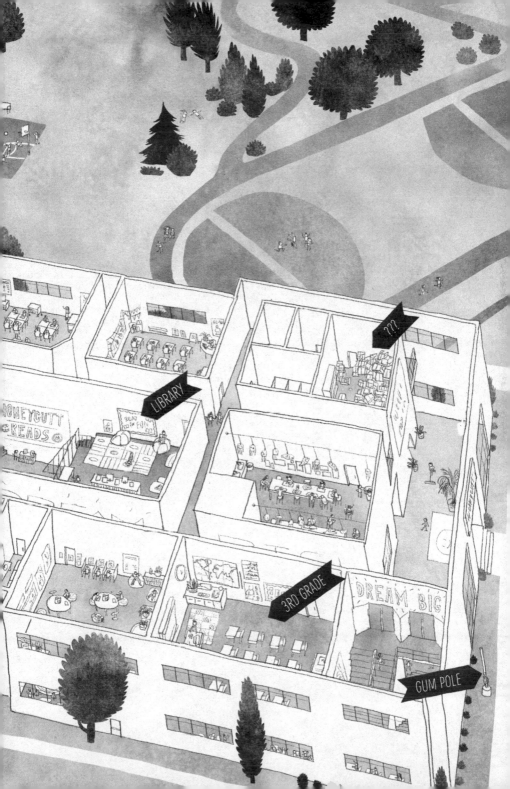

CHAPTER 1

It was definitely time to
get ready for school, but
Ben was still in bed.
It was good to be in bed.

I will stay in bed all day,
thought Ben.
I will live in this cozy, warm bed forever.

Ben's stomach made a sound like a dying hyena. He remembered the problem with staying in bed.

I want sausages, he thought. *And I want them right now.*

Ben jumped out of bed faster than a sneeze jumps out of a nose.

He wriggled out of his pajamas and into his clothes. He sprinted down the stairs and into the kitchen and almost knocked over his mom.

I suppose you want sausages,

said Ben's mom. She knew Ben pretty well. He didn't answer because he didn't have to. Asking Ben if he wanted sausages was like asking a coyote if it wanted to howl.

Ben sat down at the table and picked up his fork. His mom gave him a look.

Aren't you forgetting something?

Whatever Ben had forgotten, it couldn't be as important as sausages. But then he remembered. Because he hadn't raked the leaves yesterday, he was supposed to rake them this morning. It had seemed like a good plan at the time.

But now there were sausages.

How about I rake them *after* breakfast?

That's not what we discussed.

Plus, it's going to rain soon. There's nothing worse than raking in the rain.

Ben looked at the sausages. The sausages looked at Ben. They loved each other so much.

But Ben knew better than to argue with his mom. He went outside and raked.

His stomach was not happy with the rest of him.

When Ben came back inside, his dad was sitting at the table, wiping his mouth with his napkin. The sausage plate was empty.

Ben gasped like an actor in a movie about vampires.

Oh, Ben. I'm so sorry!

said Ben's dad.

I thought you'd eaten already!

Ben could tell that his dad was actually sorry, but it didn't help *enough*.

"Have some eggs," said Ben's mom, handing him a plate. "Have some orange juice."

Orange juice and eggs were not the same as sausages. Ben's stomach was miserable and mad.

But then he smelled something else. Something sweet and buttery and warm.

Suddenly his stomach was full of hope.

Ben's eyes followed his nose to the source of the smell. *The oven light was on! His mom was wearing oven mitts!*

"Do I smell a—?"

"Not for you," said Ben's mom like a screen door slamming shut.

"But it smells like a—"

"Don't even *think* about it, mister."

Their neighbor Mrs. Ezra had been teaching Ben's mom to bake cakes, and she was starting to get the hang of it. If there was one thing Ben liked even more than sausages, it was cake.

The timer beeped. His mom opened the oven.

The cake was yellow and fluffy and perfectly shaped.

Ben picked up a fork and greeted that cake like a seal greets a bucket of fish heads.

"Benjamin Alexander Yokoyama," said Ben's mom, and that was the end of her sentence.

Ben had once won a contest for having the name with the most syllables of any boy on his first-grade field trip to the apple orchard. It was something he was proud of.

But that wasn't why his mom had said his full name.

She'd said it so she wouldn't also have to say,

If you touch this cake with that fork, you will regret it until you are one hundred and seven years old.

I wasn't going to eat it,

said Ben. He put down the fork. He smiled at his mom like a mouse smiles at a python.

I am awfully glad to hear it, Ben. Because this cake is not for you. This cake is for ladies who ride motorcycles.

Ben's mom was in a motorcycle club that met on Monday evenings.

That's why I definitely won't eat the cake when I get home from school this afternoon.

Ben hoped that saying the words out loud would somehow make them true.

Ben's dad was putting on his coat. Ben looked at the clock. It was time to leave for school.

His mom handed him his lunch box.

"Thanks," said Ben. His stomach was already making sinister cake-eating plans. *Cut it out,* said Ben to his stomach. But Ben's stomach didn't have ears.

He had an idea. "You know what might make it easier for me to *not* eat that cake?"

Ben's mom put her hands on her hips. "You mean other than the fact that you already promised not to?"

"Yes, other than that."

"What?"

"If I could have *dessert* in my lunch today."

"No way," said Ben's mom. "No, sir."

"I think it would really help," said Ben. "Maybe something really small, like seven gingersnaps."

Ben's mom gave Ben her *You and I have different definitions of the word "small"* face.

Dessert in his lunch might make Ben feel better about not getting any sausages,

said Ben's dad.

Ben's mom gave Ben's dad a cloudy-night look.

Ben's dad gave his mom a sunny-morning smile.

Ben's mom said, "Hrumph," and looked in the cabinet. The box of gingersnaps was empty. Ben remembered maybe accidentally eating them.

"Sorry, Ben," said his mom, who didn't seem sorry at all.

At least there's that cake, said Ben's stomach.

"Wait," said Ben's dad, picking up a brown paper bag from the counter. "I just remembered! Aunt Nora left this for you when she stopped by last night."

Ben's mom gave Ben's dad a thunderstorm face.

Ben's dad's face took out its umbrella and tried to stay dry.

Ben's mom said, "Hrumph" again, and louder this time.

Ben recognized the bag. It was from the Chinese restaurant! His dad reached in and pulled out a cookie. *A fortune cookie!*

Ben reached for the cookie, but his mom grabbed it first.

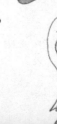

"On *one* condition," she said with her *I can't believe your dad is such a pushover* face.

"Yes?"

"Do not. Eat it. Until lunch."

"No problem," said the part of Ben that was farthest from his stomach.

Ben put his lunch box in his backpack and headed for the door.

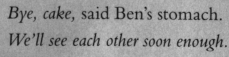

Bye, Ben,
said his dad.

Bye, Ben,
said his mom.

Bye, cake, said Ben's stomach.
We'll see each other soon enough.

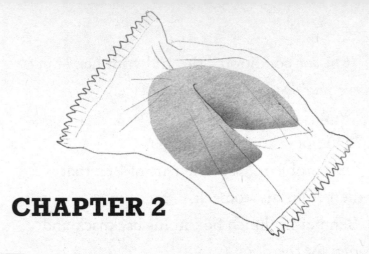

CHAPTER 2

Ben went outside. It was cloudy and cold. But not quite cold enough for snow. He walked down the front path toward the sidewalk.

So, how about that cookie? said his stomach.

Stop it,

said Ben. He was trying to do the right thing.

If we ate it under that bush over there, no one would see us, said his stomach.

Ben looked over at the bush. His stomach had a point.

He *wanted* to wait until lunch to eat the cookie. If it had been just a regular cookie, it would have been no problem. But a fortune cookie was both delicious *and* interesting, and Ben's brain was just as hungry as his stomach.

What does the fortune say?
his brain wondered. *What
wisdom does it hold?*

Ben had to know. He had to know *now*.
He crouched beneath the bush. He
pulled out his lunch box. He found the
cookie and unwrapped it.

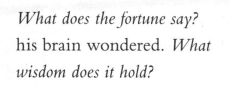

What are you doing?

Ben looked up. It was Patty
from next door. She was five and
spoke like a person who was
trying to put out a fire.

Nothing, said Ben, tucking the cookie out of sight.

That's not true, said Patty.

Why are you hiding under our bush?

Well..., said Ben, but that was as far as he got.

Patty squinted and pointed at Ben.

"What are you up to?" she asked. "People don't hide under bushes unless they're doing something sneaky."

Ben worried Patty might tell her mom. Or even worse, *his* mom. He tried a different approach.

"Usually that's true," he said, "but today I'm just eating a cookie."

Patty's eyes got happy and wide.

I like cookies.

"Would you . . . like to *share* this cookie with me?" Ben figured losing half a cookie was better than seeing his mom's tornado face.

Patty looked at the cookie and wrinkled her nose. "*That's* not a cookie."

"It is!" said Ben. "Not only is it *the most delicious cookie* in the world, but it's also *full of wisdom.*"

I want it, said Patty.

How about half?

All, said Patty, holding out her open hand.

But—

ALL! shouted Patty, with a voice like a planet exploding.

Okay! You can have the cookie, but I get to keep the fortune.

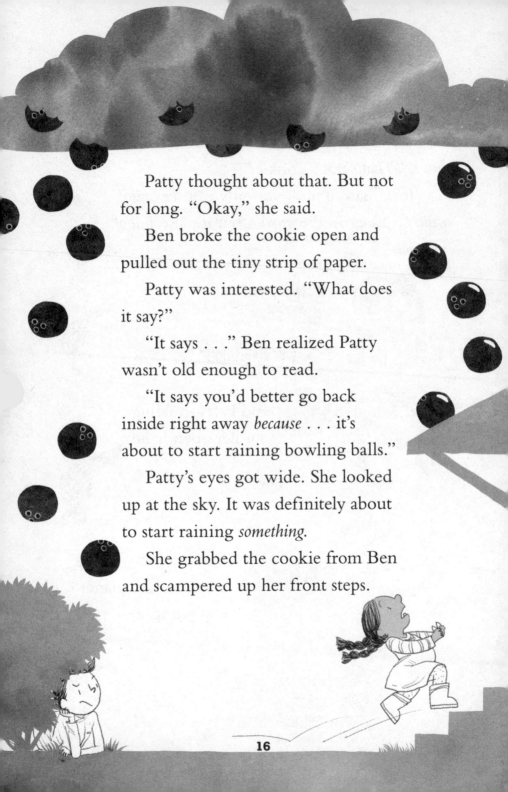

Patty thought about that. But not
for long. "Okay," she said.

Ben broke the cookie open and
pulled out the tiny strip of paper.

Patty was interested. "What does
it say?"

"It says . . ." Ben realized Patty
wasn't old enough to read.

"It says you'd better go back
inside right away *because* . . . it's
about to start raining bowling balls."

Patty's eyes got wide. She looked
up at the sky. It was definitely about
to start raining *something*.

She grabbed the cookie from Ben
and scampered up her front steps.

He looked at the fortune again.

Here's what it *actually* said:

Good things come to those who wait.

Ben gasped. It was the wisest thing he'd ever read. But he'd heard it a little too late.

If he'd waited until lunch, he wouldn't have had to give the cookie to Patty.

I'm so mad at you right now, said Ben's stomach.

Not as mad as I am at myself, said Ben.

CHAPTER 3

It started raining. Not bowling balls, but still pretty hard. Even under the bush, Ben was getting wet.

This is not a good thing, he thought.

Ben went back to his front porch. He read the fortune again.

Good things come to those who wait.

His mind went wild.
Did that mean bad things came
to those who *didn't wait?*

Or just that
good things came to
those who *did?*

Usually Ben met Janet on the corner at 8:05, but sometimes she was late. Ben didn't mind waiting on the corner by himself when it *wasn't* raining, but he minded a lot when it *was*.

It would be a good thing if Janet came and met me on the nice dry porch instead,

thought Ben.

And so he waited.

While he waited, Ben thought about other good things he wanted and had asked for but hadn't gotten yet.

- Like a brother named Ajax
- And a scooter with light-up wheels
- And eight inches of fluffy fresh snow
- And a big, bushy mustache
- And the ability to fly

All these things were good.

Ben's mom said the only way he'd ever get a brother named Ajax was by convincing some other family to adopt him. Ben was seriously considering it.

His parents had promised him a new scooter if he raked the yard once a day until all the leaves had fallen from the oak tree. Ben hadn't realized at the time that *once* a day meant the same thing as *every* day. Every day was a lot. Especially when it rained, which it had pretty much constantly since September. The sky had been so busy raining that it had forgotten how to snow.

The mustache situation was especially frustrating. Ben's uncle Earl had a mustache.

Mr. Piscarelli had a mustache.

Captain A-OK, Defender of the Improbable, had an extremely bushy mustache.

And he could fly.

It didn't seem fair.

Ben read his fortune again.

Good things come to those who wait.

A thought smacked into Ben's brain like a baseball smacks into a glove. Captain A-OK hadn't *always* had a mustache. And he'd had to graduate from Space Captain Academy before he could fly. Captain A-OK had done a whole lot of waiting.

I have spent my whole life just wanting and asking *for all these good things,* thought Ben. *I have never tried patiently* waiting *for them.*

So Ben decided to wait. Patiently. For the things he'd always wanted.

And . . . for Janet.

As 8:05 came and went, the rain fell harder. And harder. It was good to be sitting on the porch and not getting wet on the corner.

Ben waited some more.

It was 8:10.

Then 8:13.

At 8:17, Janet walked up with a scowl.

Why didn't you meet me on the corner?

Because it was raining. I thought it would be better to wait here.

Better for who?

Ben thought about that.

"Exactly!" said Janet. "I stood in the rain for five minutes!"

Ben looked at Janet. She was pretty soggy.

"Sorry," he said. "I figured you'd be late."

"I *was* late!" said Janet in the exact same way that she might have said, "I *wasn't* late!"

"So . . . I was *right* to wait on the porch?" said Ben. It was halfway between an excuse and a question.

"You didn't *know* I'd be late."

"But you *were*. That's why I didn't come to the corner."

As far as Ben was concerned, his fortune was getting smarter by the minute.

"That does not make sense!" said Janet in a voice that might technically have been a shout.

Ben considered saying, "Yes, it does," but then Janet would have said, "No, it doesn't," and then he would have had to say, "Yes, it does" again.

So Ben skipped that part and went right to the part where they walked along mad without talking.

They walked one block.

And then another.

Ben thought it would be a good thing for Janet to apologize for being late.

So he waited. But Janet didn't apologize. So he waited some more.

Eventually, they came to the corner by the school.

Well?

said Ben.

Are you going to apologize?

asked Janet. She stood there with her arms crossed like a padlock on a barbed wire fence.

"Me?" Ben was baffled. "*You're* the one who needs to apologize to *me!*"

"*I'm* the one who got soggy!"

"But I *would* have gotten soggy if I'd waited on the corner!"

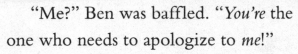

Ben and Janet were as mad as jostled ants.

The first bell rang. School would start in five minutes.

Ben looked at Janet. She had on a face that would need at least ten minutes to sort itself out.

He knew she needed time to simmer down.

He was willing to wait.

CHAPTER 4

Ben walked to his classroom.
Mr. Piscarelli and his extremely
impressive mustache were there.
　　"Today we're going to do
　　a partner project," said Mr. P.
　　"Pick partners."
Usually Ben picked Janet. But today Janet
glared at Ben like a soggy dog glares at a dry one.
　　Ben looked around and was about to pick
Kyle. But then he remembered his fortune.
　　And so he waited. Waiting made him think
about things.
　　Kyle was fun but liked to goof. Ben didn't feel
like doing all the work. But when he wasn't
goofing, Kyle could spell, and Ben was bad at
spelling.
　　Was *Kyle* the good thing?

KYLE?

JANET?

Ben had waited *some*, but he wasn't sure he'd waited *enough*.

Kyle gave Ben a *Whatever* face and picked Janet.

Janet wasn't good at spelling, either. But she did have a big vocabulary. Ben wondered what he would do without Janet's vocabulary and Kyle's spelling.

Ben panicked a little. He looked around the room. Lang didn't have a partner yet, and he knew lots of science facts.

LANG?

Was Lang the good thing?

While Ben was trying to decide, Lang picked Will.

Ben panicked a lot. He had never not picked Janet, Kyle, or Lang.

WILL!

Ben's eyes lurched around the room. Everyone seemed to have a partner. But there was an even number of kids in his class. Which meant at least one person still needed a partner.

But who?

As Ben's wondering brain asked the question, his heavy heart already knew the answer.

Nobody ever picked Walter. Walter always got whoever was left at the end of the picking.

A familiar voice crashed across the room like a boat breaking ice in a frozen harbor. Suddenly Ben's ears knew the answer also.

Ben looked. Walter was staring right at him, waving like the president was driving by. Ben tried his best but couldn't un-look. Walter's eyes were like a magnet and a vacuum cleaner in one.

"Go sit with your partners," said Mr. P.

Ben wanted to say,

No thank you.

and

Unfortunately, I'm already partners with Janet.

and

Sorry, but I have to have a cavity filled.

But none of these things was possible now. Ben had waited too long. He floated across the room like a soap bubble heading for a rosebush.

CHAPTER 5

"Hi, Ben!" shrieked Walter. Walter was always too loud.

"Hi, Walter," Ben mumbled.

"Three hundred and seventy-four days until Thanksgiving," said Walter.

"What?" said Ben. That made no sense. "There are only three hundred and sixty-five days in the year."

Correct. There are also ten days until Thanksgiving. There are also seven hundred and thirty-eight days until Thanksgiving. There are also . . .

"I get it," said Ben. Ben remembered that Walter was very good at numbers. *Maybe it will be a math project,* thought Ben. His hopes rose a little.

Is it a math project?

asked Lang.

It's not a math project, said Mr. P.

It's not an art project or a spelling project or a science project.

Ben was relieved to hear that there would be no spelling. But he was curious. What other kinds of projects were there?

Everyone was wondering, and the wondering was loud.

All right. Everybody settle down.

Everybody settled down except Walter, who usually needed to be asked twice.

"Walter!" said Mr. P. with his *Please don't make me ask you more than once* face.

Walter settled down.

"The project is a scavenger hunt," said Mr. P.

A scavenger hunt! Ben was excited!

Every once in a while, not very often, but sometimes, Mr. P.'s projects were scavenger hunts. A scavenger hunt meant looking for things and not sitting at a desk and maybe even going outside!

A scavenger hunt meant possibly winning a prize. Mr. P.'s prizes were the best.

Immediately, everyone *un*settled, especially Walter.

Mr. P. stood there not saying a word, and everyone settled again. Even Walter. A scavenger hunt was exciting, but not without the details.

"Can you tell us the details?" asked Amy Lou Bonnerman.

"I *can*," said Mr. P. But then he said nothing. Mr. P. was a stickler for the difference between "can" and "will."

"*Will* you tell us the details?" asked Amy Lou Bonnerman with her *I know you're the teacher, but I'm pretty sure you knew what I meant* face.

"I *will*," said Mr. P. with a smile. And then he did.

"In this scavenger hunt, you will hunt for *words*."

Ben was confused. Scavenger hunts were for finding *things*. Things like purple pencils or objects that rhyme with "dog" or a license plate from Tennessee.

Words were not a thing to find. *Were they?*

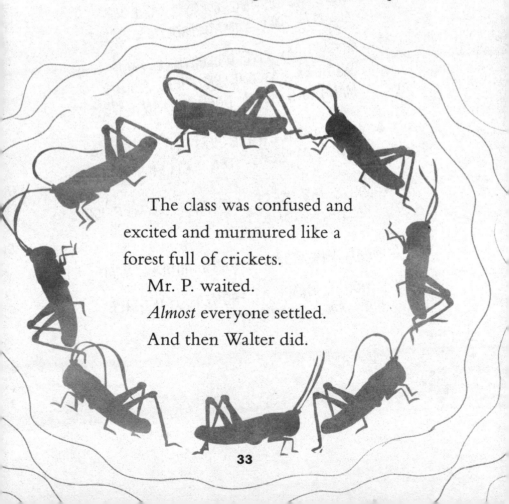

The class was confused and excited and murmured like a forest full of crickets.

Mr. P. waited.

Almost everyone settled.

And then Walter did.

Mr. P. pulled out a big sheet of poster board and set it on the chalkboard tray. This is what it said:

1. ANSWER THIS RIDDLE: WHAT IS SOMETHING THAT NEVER EXISTED IN THE PAST, YOU CAN'T HAVE TODAY, AND DISAPPEARS THE MOMENT IT ARRIVES?

2. NAME ONE OF TWO WORDS THAT HAVE ALL FIVE VOWELS IN ALPHABETICAL ORDER.

3. MEGAN HAS FIVE DAUGHTERS. EACH DAUGHTER HAS ONE BROTHER. HOW MANY CHILDREN DOES MEGAN HAVE?

4. COME UP WITH THE BEST PALINDROME THAT IS AT LEAST TEN LETTERS LONG.

5. WRITE THE BEST LIMERICK. (MR. P. WILL BE THE JUDGE.)

6. WHAT IS PRINCIPAL HOGAN'S MIDDLE NAME?

7. WHICH 3 KIDS AT HONEYCUTT HAVE THE SAME BIRTHDAY?

Ben was excited. He loved all seven questions. But he knew the answer to only one of them.

I know the answer to the riddle,

said Walter.

Really?

said Ben.

Yes.

Ben was glad. He had no idea what it was.

"What's a palindrome?" asked Lucy T.

"I'm glad you asked," said Mr. P. "A palindrome is a word, phrase, or sentence that reads the same forward and backward. For example, 'Bob.'"

"Yes?" said Bob.

"Sorry, Bob," said Mr. P. "I wasn't calling on you. I was saying that your name is a palindrome. It's *B-O-B*, whether you start at the beginning or the end."

OOOOOH!"

said the class.

Bob smiled as if he had just been handed a chocolate-covered strawberry.

"A longer example is *Madam, I'm Adam,*" said Mr. P. "And the most famous palindrome might be *A man, a plan, a canal: Panama.*"

"There's no way that reads the same forward and backward," said Kyle.

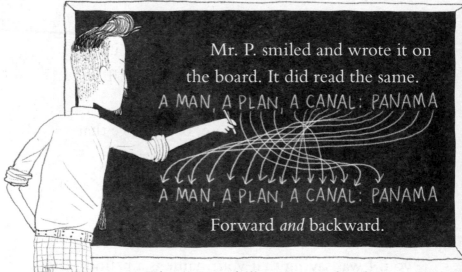

Mr. P. smiled and wrote it on the board. It did read the same.

A MAN, A PLAN, A CANAL: PANAMA

A MAN, A PLAN, A CANAL: PANAMA

Forward *and* backward.

The "Ooooh!" was even louder this time.

"Okay," said Mr. P. as he handed out the answer sheets. "As always, no looking for answers on the internet!"

Amy Lou Bonnerman waved her hand excitedly.

"Yes, Amy Lou?"

"I just want you to know that it would never even occur to me to do such a thing."

"I know, Amy Lou," said Mr. P. "And I do appreciate it."

You're welcome,

said Amy Lou, smiling
like the tiny golden
statue on top of a trophy.

Mr. P. turned to the class. "We'll work on these questions during partner time this week, and we'll do the final tally on Friday."

All week! Ben would be partners with Walter *all week!*

He wanted a do-over but knew it wasn't an option. He reminded himself that he was a nice person. He would try to make this work.

But it was going to be hard.

Walter was not like anyone else.

He said unexpected things.

I AM ZOOFARO, MASTER OF FEET!

And did unexpected things.

And wore unexpected belt buckles.

When they were in kindergarten, Walter was the best at everything. Reading. Solving puzzles. Making up games.

Ben and Walter had made up Cold Curry Catnip Kingdom, where everyone was made of pickled eggplant and anytime you got hungry you could just nibble your friend's arm and they could nibble yours. Ben used to spend Saturdays with Walter. Ben used to go to Walter's birthday parties.

But then . . .

Ben didn't know what had happened, exactly. He just didn't spend time with Walter anymore.

"Let's get started, Ben!" Walter's voice was like a swarm of mosquitoes in a world without bug spray.

Ben was feeling sorry for himself. But then he remembered his fortune.

Walter was his partner *because* he had waited. Which meant that having Walter as a partner had to be . . . *a good thing.*

It didn't make a bit of sense to Ben, but he decided to trust that the fortune knew best.

Okay, Walter.

Let's get started.

CHAPTER 6

Ben read the riddle again.

WHAT IS SOMETHING THAT NEVER EXISTED IN THE PAST, YOU CAN'T HAVE TODAY, AND DISAPPEARS THE MOMENT IT ARRIVES?

Ben had no idea. "You said you knew the answer?"

"Yes!" said Walter.

"Great," said Ben. Maybe *this* was the good thing about being Walter's partner. "What is it?"

"An invisible ostrich."

"What?!"

"Think about it. Invisible ostriches are imaginary, so they never existed in the past. And since they're invisible, you can't have them today . . . because you have no idea where they are."

Ben thought about that. It kind of made sense. *Kind* of. But the riddle had a third part, too.

"But since an invisible ostrich is *already* invisible, it can't . . . *disappear* the moment it arrives," Ben explained.

"Shucks, you're right," said Walter, who didn't seem as disappointed as Ben thought he should be.

Ben was disappointed enough for both of them.

"Let's get the easy one out of the way," said Ben.

MEGAN HAS FIVE DAUGHTERS. EACH DAUGHTER HAS ONE BROTHER. HOW MANY CHILDREN DOES MEGAN HAVE?

Oh, that *is* easy,

said Walter.

I guess Mr. P. wanted to have at least one question that *everyone* would get right,

said Ben.

He wrote *10* on their answer sheet.

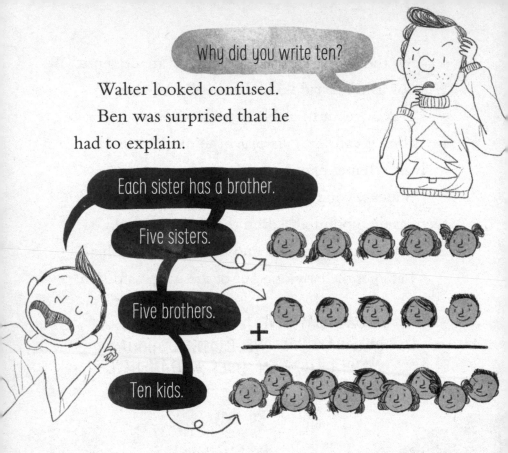

Walter looked confused.

Ben was surprised that he had to explain.

Why did you write ten?

Each sister has a brother.

Five sisters.

Five brothers.

+

Ten kids.

Walter didn't look convinced. Which worried Ben. Numbers were the one thing that Walter was supposed to be good at.

"Five plus five equals ten, right?" Ben explained.

"That's true," said Walter.

"Good," said Ben. But he wasn't feeling good.

Ben was trying his hardest to figure out how being Walter's partner was a good thing. He hadn't run out of hope yet, but he was getting close.

"What's a 'limcrick'?" asked Walter.

"A very particular kind of poem," said Ben. "They're clever and funny and fit together like a jigsaw puzzle. Here's how it works."

Ben reached into his imagination and felt around for an idea.

"There once was a . . . person named Ben. Who . . ."

Ben looked at his desk for inspiration.

Who . . . picked up a pencil and pen. With one he . . . just scribbled.

Ben used the pen to make a doodle on his paper.

The other he . . . nibbled.

Ben put his pencil sideways in his mouth and pretended to eat it.

He . . . never used . . . either again.

Ben tossed the pencil and pen over his shoulder.

Hey! said Amy Lou Bonnerman, who had just gotten bonked.

"Sorry," said Ben.

"I think you dropped these," said Mr. P., picking up the pen and pencil and handing them to Ben with his *Even coming up with an excellent limerick is no excuse for bonking your classmates with pointy objects* face.

Walter clapped and laughed. Which made Ben laugh, too.

"Who wrote that?" asked Walter.

"*I* did," said Ben. "Just now. Once you know how the rhymes work, it's easy."

Wow!

said Walter.

That's *amazing.*

The compliment felt good. Even coming from Walter. And Walter was right. Limericks *were* amazing.

Ben loved making up limericks. He loved making up rhymes. He was good at rhymes.

He was about to say "I'll write the limerick," but then he thought, *Writing the limerick is not waiting.*

"I'll take care of the limerick," said Ben. But what he meant was *I will wait, and the limerick will take care of itself.*

"Great!" said Walter. "What's next?"

"Do you know any palindromes?"

"Nope," said Walter.

"Me neither," said Ben.

They were getting nowhere.

"Pool loop!" said Walter suddenly.

"What?"

"It's a palindrome!"

Ben wrote it down.

Walter was right.

"Pool loop" read the same way forward and backward!

"I thought you didn't know any," said Ben.

"It just popped into my head," said Walter. "Snap pans!"

"What?" said Ben, but then he realized. It was another palindrome.

"Bonk knob!" said Walter.

"Shhh," said Ben. "Don't give them all away."

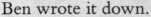

said Walter in the loudest whisper Ben had ever heard.

Ben was a little bit impressed. But none of Walter's palindromes were ten letters long. And they didn't make a bit of sense. Mr. P.'s palindromes had made sense. Ben was pretty sure that whatever palindrome was picked as the winner would need to make sense, too.

"I'll keep thinking them up," said Walter.

"Great," said Ben. "See if you can find one that's ten letters long and also makes sense."

"Got it, Ben," said Walter. "Absolutely!"

"How about the word with all the vowels?" said Ben. "Do you know it?"

"Nope," said Walter. "No idea."

Ben looked over at Janet and Kyle. They were laughing like two people who had already figured out all the answers and were busy planning their victory parade.

Being Walter's partner is a good thing, Ben reminded himself.

"What about Principal Hogan's middle name?" Ben asked. "Do you know it?"

Maybe somewhere deep in Walter's big brain was the answer to this question.

"I might," said Walter, with a thinking look on his face.

Ben let himself feel hopeful again.

"Whisper it," said Ben. "Quietly." He didn't want the other groups to hear the answer as it came booming out of Walter's megaphone mouth. Walter's eyes got wide. He leaned in.

What if it's *Gretchen?*

he whispered.

Ben was disgusted. "It's not Gretchen."

"Are you sure?" asked Walter. "How do you *know* it's not Gretchen?"

"Gretchen is a *girl's* name. Principal Hogan is a *man.*"

"My uncle's name is Leslie."

"It's *not* Gretchen!" said Ben in a not-so-quiet voice.

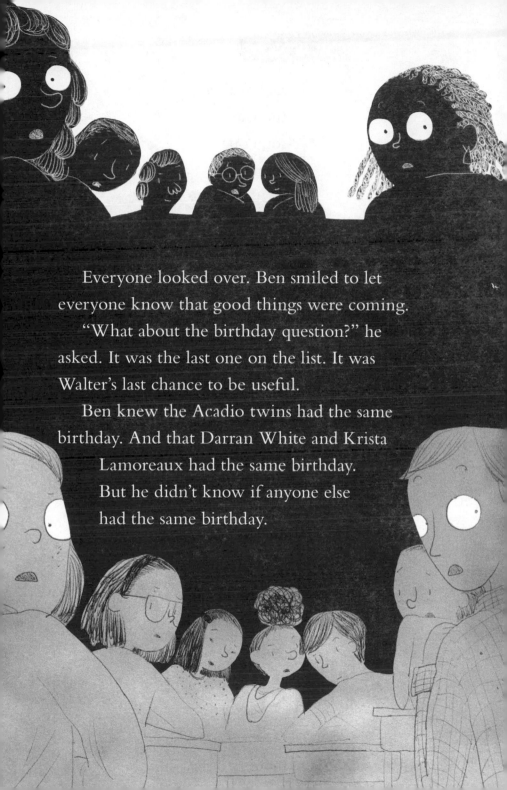

Everyone looked over. Ben smiled to let
everyone know that good things were coming.
"What about the birthday question?" he
asked. It was the last one on the list. It was
Walter's last chance to be useful.

Ben knew the Acadio twins had the same
birthday. And that Darran White and Krista
Lamoreaux had the same birthday.
But he didn't know if anyone else
had the same birthday.

Ben was trying so hard to be patient.

"Any idea which three kids in our school have the same birthday?"

"Nope," said Walter. "That's a tough one. *Your* birthday is December eighteenth."

"That's true," said Ben. He felt bad that Walter remembered. Ben hadn't invited Walter to his last two birthday parties. He wondered if Walter was mad about that.

Walter was smiling as if they were sailing on a smooth blue lake.

But the water was choppy as far as Ben could see.

They had been through all the questions and had only one answer. To the *easiest* one! The answer that probably *everyone* knew.

Everyone *except* Walter.

Ben needed Janet. Or Kyle. Or Lang. Each of them was good at *something*.

Walter was good at *nothing*.

CHAPTER 7

At lunch, Ben sat with Kyle and Lang.

Janet sat with
Emma and Kamari.

Walter sat by himself.

Walter always sat by himself. Ben
didn't want to feel bad about that.

"This scavenger hunt is weird," said Kyle.

Ben liked it better when he and Kyle liked the same things.

"I don't want to write a poem," said Lang.

"I don't want to write a poem, either," said Ben. But that wasn't true.

Ben had already written the first two lines of a limerick.

There once was a wrestler named Jake.
Who baked a spectacular cake.

But then he'd made himself stop so he could *wait* to write it instead.

"Poems are dumb," said Lang.

"The dumbest," said Kyle.

Ben said nothing. He looked over at Walter, who was writing something on a piece of paper.

Ben pulled out the fortune. Kyle and Lang didn't look at it as long as Ben wanted them to.

"I don't like waiting," said Lang. To prove it, he stopped eating his sandwich and started eating his cupcake.

Ben was suddenly glad that Lang was not his partner.

Ben felt a tap on his shoulder. He turned to look and immediately wished he hadn't.

It was Walter. Standing right beside him. Holding a piece of paper and grinning like a little kid with a lollipop.

said Walter.

Ben's face felt suddenly sunburned.

I'm pretty busy right now, said Ben.

Eating my sandwich.

Drinking my milk.

You know?

Baby carrots, too.

Ben took a big bite to show how impossible it would be to talk to Walter at that moment.

Kyle laughed and milk came out of Lang's nose.

"I can wait," said Walter. He didn't seem to be in a rush.

"It's a really big sandwich," said Ben as he chewed. "Can we talk . . . later?"

"No problem, Ben," said Walter. "See you soon."

"See you *sooooooon*," said Kyle as Walter walked away.

"Be *quiet*," said Ben. "He's nice."

"He's a weirdo," said Lang.

"He's imaginative," said Ben. It was the word Ben's mom had always used to describe Walter.

"You mean cuckoo," said Lang.

"Shut it," said Ben.

Lang did not shut it. Instead, he started talking about scooter tricks, which usually interested Ben a lot, but not today.

Walter was back at his table, still writing something.

Ben wanted to know what it was.

CHAPTER 8

Ben got up from the table and headed for the bathroom. He needed to get away from Kyle and Lang. *And* he needed to go number one.

He ran into Principal Hogan in the hallway. It seemed like a great opportunity.

"Hello, Principal Hogan," said Ben. "I have a question for you."

Hello, Ben,

said Principal Hogan.

If your question is whether I'm having a nice day, the answer is yes. But if you're planning to ask me about my middle name, I'm afraid I can't help you.

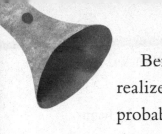

Ben was surprised, but then he
realized that every third grader had
probably been asking Principal Hogan
the same question.

"Why not?" asked Ben.

"There's a reason no one
knows my middle name."

"What's that?"

"I don't particularly like
it," said Principal Hogan. "It
does not flatter me, Ben."

"I understand why you
wouldn't want to tell the *other*
kids," said Ben, smiling at
Principal Hogan like a snake charmer smiles
at a cobra. "But you can tell *me*."

Principal Hogan looked surprised. And
interested. "And why would I do that, Ben?"

"Because me knowing your middle name
would be a good thing. Maybe you haven't
heard, but good things come to those who
wait. And I am willing to wait."

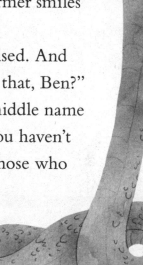

Ben pulled out the fortune and handed it to Principal Hogan.

"This is good advice," said Principal Hogan. "But I'm not sure it applies to the present situation."

Ben was disappointed. "Why not?"

"Even though knowing my middle name would be a good thing for you, it would not be a good thing for me. Which is why I don't plan to tell you."

You mean not *now*?   asked Ben.

I have no plans to tell you at any point,

said Principal Hogan.

Neither in the present,

nor in the distant future.

But it's technically possible that you might tell me eventually?

Principal Hogan looked at Ben as if Ben had three heads, six arms, twelve elbows, and a pet armadillo.

"In the same way it's technically possible for a poodle to get to the moon."

Ben smiled. He knew all you needed to get a poodle to the moon was a spaceship and lots of freeze-dried dog food.

And a poodle.

CHAPTER 9

That afternoon they did reading and writing and math. While Mr. P. explained that eating ¼ of a pizza will get you just as full as eating ⅖ of one, Ben waited patiently for all the things he wanted.

He looked out the window. It definitely didn't look like the sky before a snowstorm. He touched his upper lip. It was just as smooth as it had been at breakfast.

Ben tried not to be impatient, but it wasn't easy. He looked at the fortune to see if there was a phone number you could call to ask how long you had to wait for the good things to come.

But there wasn't.

When the last bell rang and school was over, Ben headed out to the flagpole to wait for Janet. They always walked home together. In part because they were best friends but also because their parents said they had to.

Technically, they were still having a fight. But it would be over as soon as Janet apologized. And then they could go back to normal.

When Ben got to the flagpole, Janet was already there.

Are you ready to apologize?

asked Ben.

No way!

said Janet.

Are you?

Ben *wanted* to apologize. He was tired of being mad at Janet. He was tired of Janet being mad at him.

He was also *willing* to apologize. Right after Janet did.

You first, said Ben.

 You're the one who was late.

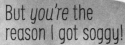  But *you're* the reason I got soggy!

That's good advice, she said, forgetting their fight for a second.

 Right?

Ben saw that he still had some work to do.

Not being soggy is a good thing. You *waited* all day, and now you're dry.

Janet thought about that.

I have to admit, that makes a little bit of sense.

 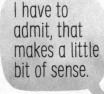

Ben suddenly realized why Janet was so confused. She hadn't had a chance to read his fortune.

Look,

he said, handing it to her.

Ben was relieved. Janet *understood*.

But I don't see what it has to do with me getting soggy.

That's true. But I wish I hadn't gotten soggy in the first place.

The only reason *I* didn't get soggy is because I *waited* on my porch.

Exactly.

Ben was glad that Janet was coming around.

"I'm going to follow this advice," said Janet, handing the fortune back to Ben.

"Great!" he said. "By apologizing?"

"No," said Janet. "By *waiting* for you to apologize to me. Because that would be a very good thing."

"Almost as good a thing as you apologizing to me!"

They stood with their arms folded, waiting like professional sloth watchers, until it started raining again.

At which point, they suddenly stopped waiting and started to scamper.

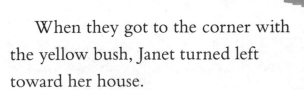

When they got to the corner with the yellow bush, Janet turned left toward her house.

Ben followed. He usually went to Janet's after school, and they usually watched *Snooptown*.

On Friday there had been a cliff-hanger involving an actual cliff. Ben couldn't wait to see whether the llama would let go of the rope.

They were halfway down the block before Janet realized that Ben was following her.

"What are you doing?" she snapped.

"Coming over," said Ben. "To watch *Snooptown*. The *cliff-hanger!*"

"No way," said Janet. "Not until you apologize."

"But . . . ending this fight and watching *Snooptown* are both good things. That means they'll only happen if I *wait*."

That's ridiculous.

Janet was revved up like a chainsaw.

Let me tell you something. Those good things will only happen if you apologize.

Now.

Ben wanted to do it. He really did. But doing something now was the opposite of waiting.

He played the last card in his hand.

"But if I don't come over, we can't watch *Snooptown*."

"That's true," said Janet. "*We* can't. But *I* can."

"*Without* me?"

Without you. And I'm going to sit right in the middle of the big blue chair.

Ben wanted to shout forbidden words.

The big blue chair was so big that both of them could sit next to each other without their shoulders even touching. Sitting in the middle was an insult.

Apologize, Ben.

Janet's eyes got soft and wide, like they were saying please.

It's easy.

"Not as easy as waiting."

Janet made an awful sound and stomped away.

Ben watched her go. At that moment, waiting was the hardest thing in the world.

CHAPTER 10

Ben went back home, and there was the cake.

He had forgotten about the cake.

His stomach had not forgotten.

Ben tried to figure out how to eat some cake without his mom knowing that he'd eaten it.

Certain kinds of cake could be secretly nibbled. But not this one. Even the slightest nibble would be noticed.

Darn you, you perfect cake, thought Ben. Then he felt bad. It was not the cake's fault that it was perfect.

Sorry, cake, thought Ben.

Then he remembered! *This cake is a good thing. If I wait, it will come to me.*

While he was waiting,
Ben tried reading *Captain
A-OK and the Pan-Galactic
Sneeze,* but all he could
think about was cake.

Then he tried
riding his scooter, but
all he could think
about was cake.

So he raked the leaves,
which were wet and
heavy. He couldn't
believe how many had
fallen since this morning.

When Ben came back inside, he was soggy.
At least there's that cake, said his stomach.

But his stomach was wrong. As soon as his
mom got home from work, she took the cake to
her meeting and Ben got none.

He looked at his fortune. He tried to make sense of things.

Maybe the motorcycle ladies won't eat all the cake, Ben thought. *Maybe I'll get some later.*

His mom came home with an empty plate.

Come on, Fortune, thought Ben.

He was getting a little discouraged. First he hadn't gotten to watch *Snooptown*. Now he was missing out on cake.

"Hey, Ben," said Ben's mom. "I'm proud of you for not eating the cake earlier. So I stopped at the store on the way home and picked up a little something."

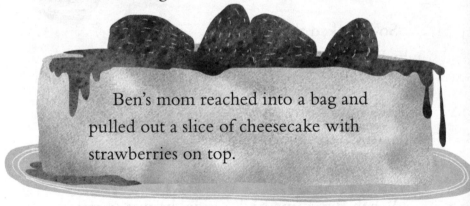

Ben's mom reached into a bag and pulled out a slice of cheesecake with strawberries on top.

"Are you hungry?" asked Ben's mom. Ben didn't answer. He didn't have to. Asking Ben if he was hungry for cheesecake was like asking a bug bite if it wanted to be scratched.

After the cheesecake and homework and some reading with his dad, Ben got in bed. Before he went to sleep, he took out his fortune.

I'm sorry I doubted you,

Ben thought.

He drifted off to sleep, thinking about all the other good things that were headed his way.

CHAPTER 11

The next morning, Ben looked in the mirror. He couldn't tell for sure, but his upper lip seemed just a tiny bit fuzzier than it had the day before. *Not much longer now,* he thought.

He sprinted down the stairs and into the kitchen and almost knocked over his mom.

"I suppose you want some sausages?" she asked, handing him a plate.

"Hello, sausages," said Ben.

I waited for you. And here you are. And you are good.

Ben looked out the window and noticed that many more leaves had fallen in the night. They looked heavy and wet. It occurred to him how good it would be if someone else raked them.

It was not raining, so Ben waited on the corner. Janet was right on time.

Hi, said Ben.

Hi, said Janet.

They stood there for a second, both of them waiting for someone to apologize.

But no one did. So they walked to school in silence.

Ben wanted to ask Janet all about the scavenger hunt. He wanted to share the first two lines of his limerick. He wanted to tell her how "invisible ostrich" was almost-but-not-quite the perfect answer to the riddle.

But the only words Janet wanted to hear were the only words Ben was not willing to say.

Ben waited and waited, and eventually it was time to work on the scavenger hunt.

"Sit with your partners," said Mr. P.

Where Walter should have been was the fattest book Ben had ever seen.

"Hi, Ben." Walter popped out from behind the book. He was grinning like someone who had just sipped a milkshake.

"Is that the dictionary?" Ben asked.

"Not just any dictionary. The *unabridged* dictionary. It has *all* the words."

Walter was excited. Walter was proud.

"Where did you get it?"

"The school library. Mrs. Piendak says I'm the first student who ever checked it out."

Ben could believe it. The book was the size of a small suitcase.

"It weighs twelve pounds," said Walter.

"How do you know that?"

"Mrs. Piendak told me. There are 450,000 definitions inside."

Ben remembered. Walter had always loved knowing how many of something there were. The number of stars in the sky, the number of bones in a buffalo, the number of stairs in the Leaning Tower of Pisa.

"Why do you have it?"

"Scavenger hunt question number two. Both of the words with all five vowels in order are in here *somewhere*."

Ben thought about that. The words *were* in there. *Somewhere*. It *was* exciting. But it was also hopeless. It would be like trying to find a specific starfish in the whole wide ocean.

How in the world are you going to find them?

"I am going to read this book," said Walter, as if the answer were obvious.

"You're going to *read* it?"

"Yes," said Walter, "from the very beginning. To the very end. Or until I find our words."

"But it's hundreds of pages long!"

It's 2,662 pages.

I started this morning. The first word was "aardvark." And the last word is "Zyzzogeton." I checked. Somewhere between them are our words.

I will find them, Ben. You can count on me.

Ben thought about that. Walter was loud. He was unpredictable. But he had never let Ben down.

Walter always showed up when he said he would. He never laughed when Ben fell down. When Walter said he would do something, he did it. If anyone could find those words, it was Walter.

"Great," said Ben, who suddenly felt sorry that there were so many words in the world.

AARDVARK

ZYZZOGETON

Whatever the mysterious words turned out to be, Ben hoped they were closer to "aardvark" than to "Zyzzogeton."

"More good news!" said Walter. "I solved the riddle."

"Really?" Ben was excited. He leaned in close. "What's the answer? Remember to *whisper* the answer so nobody hears you."

said Walter in a whisper you could have heard in Australia.

"Whisper even quieter," Ben suggested.

asked Walter in a whisper you could have heard in France.

"Pretend like I'm sitting right across the desk from you," said Ben.

Okay. How's this?

said Walter in a whisper that was almost quiet enough to not wake up a sleeping rhinoceros.

WUT?

Ben assumed it was the best that Walter could do.

"Fine. So what's the answer?"

"The president's breakfast." Walter's eyes were as wide as a dinosaur's yawn.

"What?!"

Think about it. The president's breakfast isn't the *president's* breakfast until the moment you give it to her, so it never existed in the past.

You definitely can't have it now because it belongs to the president.

And it disappears the second it arrives because she's so hungry that she eats it right away.

Walter was smiling like he'd just found a dollar on the sidewalk.

"Um. That definitely *could* be it," said Ben. "But just in case that's *not* it, maybe we should keep thinking of *other* answers, too."

"Okay!" said Walter.

Ben wondered what it would take to make him stop smiling.

"What about the questions you've been working on?" asked Walter.

Ben thought about saying that he'd been waiting as hard as he could for the answers to come. But he also wanted it to sound like he'd been actually *doing* something in the meantime.

"Principal Hogan is going to tell me his middle name."

"Great!" said Walter. "When?"

"I'm not sure yet," said Ben. "We have to be patient."

"Okay," said Walter. "Will it be by Friday?"

Ben thought about that. It would only be a good thing if Principal Hogan told him by Friday. Which meant that . . .

"He absolutely will."

"Great," said Walter.

"How about the palindrome?" said Ben. "Any progress?"

"Yes," said Walter with a proud smile on his face.

Ben was impressed. *Go dog* read the same forward and backward. And it actually made sense. But it wasn't ten letters long.

"Good work," he said. "See if you can make it a little bit longer."

"All right!" said Walter. "I will."

"How about the birthday question?" Ben asked.

"I'm working on a Great Big Plan," said Walter. "I just have to figure out the details."

Ben remembered. Walter had always made Great Big Plans.

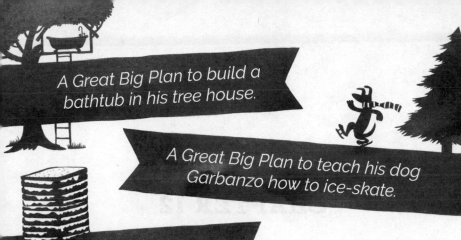

A Great Big Plan to build a bathtub in his tree house.

A Great Big Plan to teach his dog Garbanzo how to ice-skate.

A Great Big Plan to make a ten-layer PB&J.

Walter's Great Big Plans often didn't seem like good ideas, and they sometimes made a huge mess, but somehow they usually worked out in the end.

Ben's heart felt the slightest shimmer of hope.

Walter sat there reading the dictionary.

Ben sat there trying not to write his limerick.

His brain sat there not cooperating with that plan.

There once was a boy with a scooter,
Who wanted a better computer.

Stop it, said Ben.

I won't, said Ben's brain.

Ben's brain had a mind of its own.

CHAPTER 12

It was raining again when school ended, so Ben and Janet scampered along the sidewalk, still not apologizing.

When they got to the corner with the yellow bush, Janet went her way and Ben went his.

Ben was almost home when he saw a wasabi pea moving slowly across the sidewalk.

His first thought was *I love wasabi peas!* and his second thought was *I have never seen a wasabi pea that knew how to walk.*

He looked closer and saw that the wasabi pea was on top of an ant, who was working extremely hard to move it from one place to someplace else.

Ben looked around to see if he could find out where the wasabi pea had come from, but it was a mystery.

He was amazed and impressed and wanted to help the ant, but he also knew it wasn't necessary. The ant was doing just fine.

Ben wanted to show the ant to Janet so that they could be amazed and impressed together. He wanted to ask her whether she thought the ants would burn their mouths on the wasabi pea when they tried to eat it. He wanted to remind her of the time they had eaten so many wasabi peas that they had gotten runny noses.

But Janet wasn't there.

When Ben got home, there was no cake. Instead, there was an apple. And a note.

Ben —
You might want to rake the leaves right away. It's supposed to rain this afternoon.
Mom ☺

Too late, thought Ben. He went outside. Once again, the yard was completely covered with leaves.

And yet, when he looked up into the branches of the oak tree, there were still more leaves than Ben could imagine raking in a lifetime.

Please fall all at once, he thought, *so we can get this over with.*

But clearly the tree preferred to make Ben wait.

It would be a good thing if these soggy leaves were already raked and stuffed into a plastic bag, thought Ben.

He decided to wait for this good thing to happen.

Eventually, the rain stopped. Instead of raking the leaves, Ben sat on the back porch and pondered life's great mysteries.

How were the leaves going to get raked
without him doing the raking?

Maybe a sudden wind would blow them
into one neat pile?

Maybe leprechauns would eat them at midnight?

Are leprechauns real? Ben wondered. *And do
they eat leaves?*

"Hi." A voice cut through the soggy gloom.

It was one of Ben's favorite voices in the
world. It was exactly the voice that he wanted to
hear at that moment.

Ben turned in the direction of the voice and
saw Janet's head poking up above the tall fence
that separated his yard from hers.

But only for a moment, because then she was
gone.

And then she was back again.

Then gone again.

Ben knew what was happening.
There was a trampoline in Janet's backyard.

I . . .

have . . .

an idea,

said Janet as
she bounced.

Ben couldn't help but
smile. Stringing
together what Janet
was trying to say was
so much better than
waiting for the leaves
to rake themselves.

Great!

said Ben. Janet's ideas
were usually pretty good.

"Can I . . . come over . . . and tell you . . . in
person?" Janet spoke like a robot whose batteries
are running low.

"I . . .

think . . .

you should."

Ben built his sentence one stone at a time as Janet bounced up and down.

Janet stopped bouncing. A moment later, her head appeared at the top of the ladder her mom had recently installed so that Janet wouldn't have to walk all the way around the block every time she wanted to visit Ben.

Janet cleared her throat. Whatever she had to say was apparently very important.

I am waiting for the good thing that is you apologizing,

said Janet.

You are waiting for the good thing that is me apologizing.

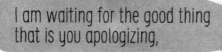

Yep,

said Ben.

That's the situation we're in.

"Your fortune is pretty wise," said Janet, "but I once got a different fortune that said, 'Two wrongs don't make a right.'"

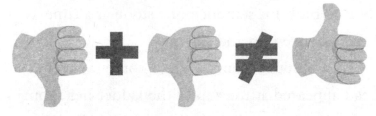

"What does that mean?"

"It means that when someone does something that makes you mad, doing something to make them mad doesn't actually make you feel better. It just means twice as many people are mad."

"Hmm," said Ben. "Like when you bake a cake that tastes terrible, instead of using the same batter to bake another terrible cake, you should mix up new batter and try again?"

"Sort of," said Janet.

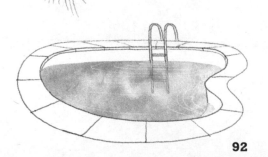

"So your idea has something to do with cake?" Ben was hopeful like a swimming pool in summer.

"Not at all," said Janet. Ben was disappointed like a snowman when springtime comes.

Janet climbed over the fence and dropped down into Ben's yard.

"Here's my idea. How about instead of both of us waiting to apologize, which is kind of like two wrong things, *neither* of us waits, which is kind of like throwing out the bad cake batter, and we *both* apologize now?"

Ben thought about that. It sounded pretty good, except for the part about not waiting.

"How about this," Ben suggested, looking at his watch. "What if we both wait for exactly one minute and then apologize at the exact same time?"

Janet thought about that.

"Works for me," she said.

They stood there peering at Ben's watch as a full sixty seconds crawled by. It was the longest minute of their lives.

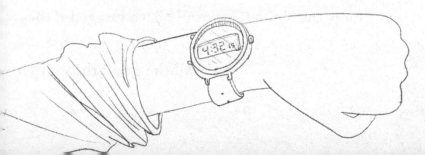

When it was finally over, they

It was a moment when they would have hugged if they
stood there, feeling glad that the
all the good things that

both spoke at the very same time.

I'm sorry I was late.

I forgive you.

I missed you.

were the kind of friends who hugged. Instead, they
fight was over and looking forward to
were suddenly possible again.

"Do you want some help with these leaves?" Janet knew all about Ben's scooter-leaf plan.

"That would be great."

Janet raked and Ben scooped the leaves into the bag.

"So . . ." Ben wanted to know how things were going with Kyle but didn't want to have to *ask*.

Things are okay with Kyle,

said Janet, who could have made a fortune as a professional mind reader.

How did you—?

But instead of answering the question Ben was asking *now,* Janet moved on to answering the one he would have asked *next.*

"Kyle is pretty smart and he's really good at spelling, but he isn't you. He didn't say thanks when I gave him a gumball. He doesn't appreciate a well-sharpened pencil. Honestly, Ben, I wish you were my partner. But since you're not, I'm making the best of it."

Ben's heart felt warm
and full and deeply
relieved, like it had been
underwater for way too
long and had just had
the chance to take a gulping breath.

He didn't know whether to say *Thank you* or
I'm sorry, so instead he said, "Me too."

There was a great long rumble of thunder.

"How are things with Walter?" asked Janet,
lifting a big pile of wet leaves into the bag.

"Good," said Ben, trying to make it sound
true. "Perfect."

"That's great," said Janet. She raked a little
more and said, "Because it seemed like you
might be a little . . . frustrated."

Even when there was a way to walk
around a big puddle of something
uncomfortable, Janet usually preferred to wade
right into the muck.

For whatever reason, Ben decided to join her.

"Walter and I used to be friends," said Ben.
"Best friends, maybe." First, he felt
embarrassed for admitting it, and then he
felt guilty for feeling that way.

But Janet didn't seem surprised.

"What happened?"

"I've been trying to figure that out."

Ben hoped Janet might know.
She knew so many other things.
But instead, she kept raking while
Ben kept on thinking out loud.

I guess we both . . .
changed.

Or else I changed
and Walter didn't.

Or maybe *he* changed and *you* didn't?

Janet suggested,
covering all the bases.

"Maybe," said Ben. But he didn't
think that was it. Walter had always
been Walter, full of overwhelming
*Walter*ness. But Ben was
definitely different than he'd
been in kindergarten when he
and Walter spent all their time
together. He just didn't know
if he'd changed for the better.

Janet kept raking as
Ben thought it over.

You're right,

Ben said, finally.

I *am* frustrated. But according to my fortune, there must be a good thing that will come from being Walter's partner.

Janet could tell Ben was trying to pick an apple he couldn't quite reach.

I get the sense that he'd do anything for you.

Yeah,

said Ben.

Janet was probably right.

Which is not worth nothing.

Ben thought about that. Walter's friendship was worth a whole lot more than nothing.

When they were finally done raking, they
were both kind of soggy.

"Want to come over until your parents get
home?"

"Yes!"

There was no ladder on Ben's side of the
fence, because they didn't need one.

They climbed the oak tree, crawled out
onto the big limb that reached over into Janet's
yard, and dropped down onto the trampoline.

They went inside and made hot chocolate.
Janet loaned Ben a dry shirt.

They got the thickest quilt and sat side by
side on the big blue chair. *Snooptown* was just
beginning.

CHAPTER 13

After *Snooptown,* Ben went home.

Once again, the fortune had been right. Ben had waited to rake the leaves, and someone had shown up to help him. Ben had waited to apologize, and now he and Janet were friends again.

But so far, waiting for the perfect palindrome to jump into his head *hadn't* worked.

Ben decided to wait . . . *harder.*

He got a piece of paper and sat down at the table. He waited and waited, but the paper stayed empty.

Any day now, thought Ben.

I've got nothing, said his brain.

Wow!

said Ben's mom.

She was looking out the kitchen window at the backyard. "That's the best raking you've ever done, Ben."

But Ben only halfway heard.

"What did you say?"

"I said you did a really good job raking."

"No, before that. You said, 'Wow.'"

"Yes, I did. It's a thing that people say when they're surprised."

Ben's mind clicked like a switch.

"'Wow' . . . is a palindrome!"

"It certainly is," said Ben's dad, who had just walked into the room.

Ben wrote it down.

W<u>O</u>W

"Turn your paper upside down," said Ben's dad.

"What do you mean?" Ben asked.

"Just try it."

Ben did. Now the <u>paper</u> said,

MOM

"'Mom' . . . is *also* a palindrome!" said Ben.

"I beg your pardon?" said Ben's mom, pretending to be offended. She gave Ben a kiss on the top of his head.

"I'm glad to see that Mr. P. has you so excited about words," said Ben's dad.

But Ben wasn't listening. He was onto something big.

WOW, MOM, WOW

It was an amazing palindrome! And it even sort of made sense! And . . .

"Ugh!" said Ben.

"What's the problem?" his dad asked.

"My palindrome is only nine letters long. It has to be at least *ten* letters long."

"So you just need to add a word at the beginning and end," said Ben's dad.

Ben's dad was right. He usually was.

"We have to get ready," said his mom.

"We're going dancing," said his dad. "Aunt Nora is coming over to have dinner with you."

Ben didn't hear them. He was waiting for other palindromes to pop into his head.

While he waited, he looked around the kitchen.

There was the salt. "Salt" was not a palindrome.

There was a bowl of apples. "Apple" was not a palindrome.

There was Dumbles eating a leftover pork chop. Ben's parents had a rule that Dumbles wasn't supposed to eat people food, but Ben's mom was really bad at following it.

"Dumbles" was not a palindrome.

"Pork chop" was not a palindrome.

But . . .

Ben's brain leaned forward, teetering on the very edge of greatness.

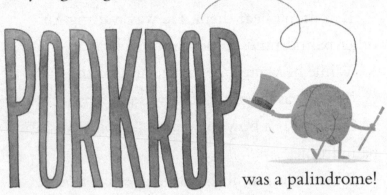 was a palindrome!

Ben's brain did a backflip and took a deep bow.

Ben told his brain to hold on for a second.

Is "porkrop" even a word? he wondered.

He was pretty sure he'd heard someone say "porkrop" before. He thought a porkrop might be some kind of coat you wore in extremely cold places.

I told you so, said Ben's brain.

First Ben apologized to his brain for doubting it and then thanked it for being so smart.

PORKROP WOW MOM WOW PORKROP

was so much more than ten letters. And even though it didn't make a lot of sense, it made *some* sense. At least a *little*.

Or, thought Ben, *even if it made no sense at all, it was still extremely fun to say.*

Ben was sure it would be the best palindrome.

If "porkrop" was actually a word. *If.*

Ben got out his dictionary. "Porkrop" was not a word.

At least not yet, thought Ben, whose brain was like a cork that simply wouldn't sink.

If "porkrop" didn't mean anything in particular, that meant it could mean anything at all!

Ben tried to figure out what "porkrop" might mean.

Maybe "porkrop" is the opposite of "mustache," thought Ben.

He felt his upper lip, wondering how much longer it would be "porkrop."

Who gets to make up new words? Ben wondered. He figured it must be someone's job.

Ben took out his notebook and wrote *Person Who Makes Up New Words* beneath *Scooter Trick Inventor* and *Cake Quality Inspector* on his "List of Things to Be When I Grow Up."

The doorbell rang.

"Hi, Nora," said Ben's mom.

"Bye, Ben," said Ben's dad.

Nora had brought lo mein and wonton soup. Lo mein was number three on Ben's list of favorite noodles, right after udon and spaghetti. Wontons were like a present filled with sausage that was deliciously bundled in noodle wrapping paper. It was probably the perfect food.

Thank you! said Ben.

I had to, said Nora.

You're my favorite nephew.

Ben was Nora's only nephew.

"So what's new, Benjabod?"

"We're doing a scavenger hunt at school."

"Oh yeah? What are you scavenging for?"

"Words."

"Like what?"

"Like . . . do you happen to know a word with all five vowels in alphabetical order?"

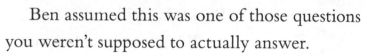

Do I look like a dictionary?

Ben assumed this was one of those questions you weren't supposed to actually answer.

"What else?" said Nora.

"Do you want to hear the easy one?"

"My favorite kind."

"Megan has five daughters. Each daughter has one brother. How many kids does Megan have?"

"Ten," said Nora, without missing a beat.

"I told you it was easy."

"Okay," said Nora. "Give me a hard one."

"We have to figure out our principal's middle name, but he won't tell us what it is."

Nora looked interested.

"Who's your principal?"

"Buck Hogan."

Nora gasped.

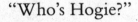

You can't mean . . . Hogie?

"Who's Hogie?"

"Your Principal, Buckminster Hogan. We went to Honeycutt together."

"You did?"

"We were in the same class. He went by Hogie, because who wants to go by Buckminster?"

"Do you remember his middle name?"

"*Yes!* It was completely ridiculous. It was . . . it was . . ." But Nora couldn't remember. "Sorry."

Nora's phone rang. "I have to take this," she said.

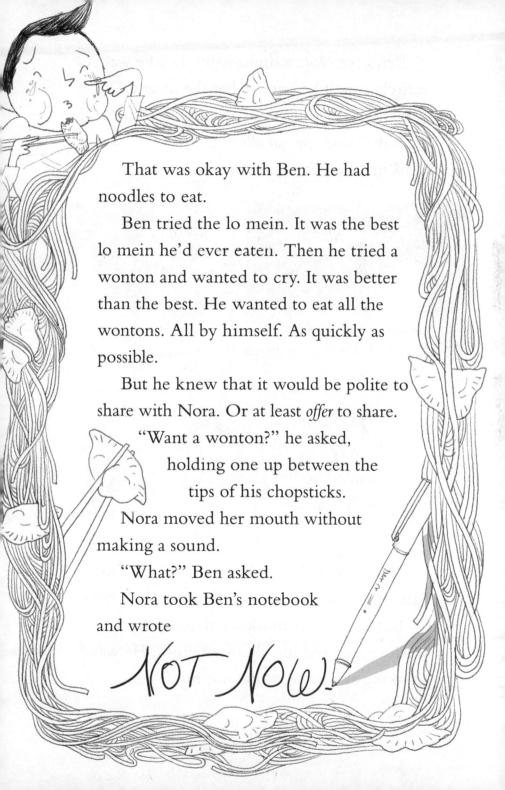

That was okay with Ben. He had noodles to eat.

Ben tried the lo mein. It was the best lo mein he'd ever eaten. Then he tried a wonton and wanted to cry. It was better than the best. He wanted to eat all the wontons. All by himself. As quickly as possible.

But he knew that it would be polite to share with Nora. Or at least *offer* to share.

"Want a wonton?" he asked, holding one up between the tips of his chopsticks.

Nora moved her mouth without making a sound.

"What?" Ben asked.

Nora took Ben's notebook and wrote

NOT NOW!

Ben gave Nora a thumbs-up. But he wasn't entirely sure if he knew what she meant. Did Nora mean that she wanted a wonton *later* or that she didn't want one *at all*?

While Ben wondered, he ate wontons.

"Not *now*, Ben," said Nora, out loud this time. She stood up and left the room in a huff.

But Ben wasn't thinking about Nora. He wasn't even thinking about wontons. He was thinking about the *words* "not now" and "wonton."

Ben gasped. He lunged across the room and got a pencil.

He wrote "wonton" next to Nora's "not now."

NOT NOW, WONTON.

It was a palindrome!
It was more than ten letters long!
And it made sense!
Sort of.
At least, it made a lot more sense than

PORKROP WOW MOM WOW PORKROP

Ben's heart lurched forward like the goose that just got invited to fly at the point of the V.

Apparently, Ben was good at palindromes.

He couldn't wait to tell Walter.

CHAPTER 14

That night Ben dreamed about flying.
It was so wonderful and vivid that
when he woke up he was sure it
was real, that the waiting had worked,
and that he'd never have to walk
anywhere again. He stood on
the edge of his bed and
leaped into space like an
eagle with a jet pack.

He crashed to the floor like a baby sloth with slippery fingers.

Ben stood up and checked the parts of him that hurt. Nothing was broken, not even his patience. One morning he would wake up and fly. He just hadn't waited long enough.

Instead of flying to breakfast, Ben sprinted down the stairs and into the kitchen and almost knocked over his dad.

At breakfast, Ben didn't mention how patiently he had been waiting for Ajax, because he knew he didn't have to. His dad gave his mom a great big hug. *It was only a matter of time.*

Ben's mom went off to work, leaving Ben and his dad both staring at the last sausage.

"Half and half?" his dad suggested.

"Sure," said Ben. It seemed fair to him. But not at all to his stomach.

Ben looked at his dad and had a shocking thought.

"Why don't *you* have a mustache?" His dad's upper lip was smooth as the surface of a bubble.

"I don't want one."

"Why not?"

"I tried growing one once. It was way too tickly."

Ben was not convinced.

"I want one," he said. "A lot."

Ben's dad smiled. "Good news and bad news," he said.

"Good news first," said Ben, who always preferred to start with dessert.

"You will absolutely have a mustache if you want one. You couldn't stop it if you tried."

"That *is* good news," said Ben. "What's the bad news?"

"Your mustache won't come until it's good and ready. There's no way to rush it. You just have to wait."

"Like with Ajax," said Ben.

"Not at all like Ajax!" said Ben's dad, laughing. "You can wait and wait as long as you like and might never have a little brother. *That's* beyond your control. But you *will* eventually grow a mustache. Though you might change your mind and decide to shave it off when the time comes and you see how tickly it is."

Never, said Ben, who had never been more certain of anything.

We'll see, said his dad with a smile.

They finished their breakfasts. Ben's stomach was full of sausages. His head was full of questions.

"Do you remember Walter?"

"Of course," said his dad. "He was very imaginative."

"Do you remember why we stopped being friends? Did we have a fight or something?"

Ben's dad thought about that. "Not that I remember."

But Ben needed more.

"Can't you remember anything at all?"

Ben's dad reached out and touched Ben's shoulder.

"It's funny," he said. "Sometimes we don't realize that things have ended until they've been over for a while. So we don't pay as much attention as we wish we had. I can't remember the last time I changed your diaper, for example."

"Stop!"

"It's true!" his dad said, laughing. "And I can't remember the last time you fell asleep in my lap. If I had known it was the last time, I definitely would have tried to remember every detail."

Ben's dad looked both happy and sad, which is kind of how Ben felt when he thought about Walter.

Ben's dad gave Ben's shoulder a squeeze.

"What I remember is the *first* time you did certain things. Like the first time you ate a noodle. I think you were one and a half."

"What did I do?"

"You got the biggest smile I have ever seen on the face of a human being."

"I did?" Ben smiled.

"And then you demanded more and more and howled when we finally cut you off because we worried that you might explode."

"Makes sense," said Ben, feeling sorry for his one-year-old self.

And I remember the first time you got on a scooter.

What did I do?

You were barely big enough to reach the handles, but you loved it so much that you stuck with it all afternoon until you figured it out.

Ben tried to picture the younger version of himself, but it was hard to imagine being anything other than exactly what he was.

"But my favorite memory is how excited you were the day you met Janet."

"Tell me."

"You came home on the first day of second grade and told us you'd just met *the apple of your eye*."

"I did?"

"You did!" his dad said with a laugh. "You must have heard that phrase somewhere. Your mom and I couldn't stop laughing. And then we found out that she lived right on the other side of the fence."

Ben smiled big, remembering how excited he'd been to discover that his new friend Janet was only an oak tree away.

But then he remembered his original question and frowned.

"Nothing else about Walter and me?"

"Sorry, Ben," said his dad. "Sometimes people just stop being friends, and it's nobody's fault."

Ben knew his dad was trying to make him feel better, but it wasn't the answer he was looking for. In his experience, things that went wrong were always *somebody's* fault, and he wanted to know who to blame.

Even if the answer
ended up being himself.

CHAPTER 15

Ben and Janet were walking to school.

Ben wanted to know how many questions Janet and Kyle had answered so far, but he didn't want to have to *ask*.

"Kyle and I have answered two questions," said Janet like a firecracker that goes off before you even light the fuse.

Ben was amazed. And also relieved. He had assumed it would be at least five.

How about you and Walter?

Two,

he said.

Cool,

said Janet.

"Look!" said Ben.
There was the ant again,
with another wasabi pea.

"Impressive," said
Janet. "Did you know
that ants can carry 5,000
times their own weight?"

"That's amazing," said Ben.

"It really is," said Janet.

They watched the ant so long that they were
almost late for school. It was absolutely worth it.

Ben wanted to be friends with Janet
forever, or maybe even longer, if he could.

The morning flew by. Then it was lunch. "Partner time until gym," said Mr. P. when the class got back from lunch.

Ben walked over to Walter's desk. He found Walter behind the enormous dictionary.

"I have a palindrome," said Ben with a smile.

"You do?" Walter was excited.

"I do," said Ben. He was excited, too.

"What is it?"

Ben paused. He wanted to tell Walter because he was excited and proud, but he didn't want to tell Walter because Walter was like a safe with the combination printed on its door.

It's very important that we keep it **TOP-SECRET.**

Of course.

Ben could tell that Walter was willing to try. He just wasn't sure that, in Walter's case, being willing was quite *enough*.

"Maybe I should write it down so no one accidentally overhears us."

"Good idea."

Ben made a little wall out of books and wrote down:

NOT NOW, WONTON

Walter's eyes got wide. He opened his mouth. Ben knew what was about to come out.

"Not now—" Walter simply couldn't help himself.

Ben clapped his hand over Walter's mouth.

"Top-secret," said Ben, taking his hand away.

"Top-secret," said Walter, pointing excitedly at the palindrome the way a scientist might point at an actual unicorn.

IT'S AMAZING! said Walter with a shout that rattled the windows, but Ben didn't mind the other kids hearing that part.

"Oh man, Ben. You're so smart," said Walter. The compliments were taking some of the sting out of Ben's frustration.

"Now we have answers for two questions," said Ben. "The brothers and the palindrome. I'm working on the limerick and Principal Hogan's middle name."

"That's good," said Walter.

"I happen to know that Janet and Kyle also have two answers."

"Good for them," said Walter.

"No, I mean they *only* have two questions answered so far. We're still tied."

"Oh," said Walter. "Got it."

But Walter did not seem to actually get it. Being tied wasn't good enough. They needed

MORE POINTS
in order to

WIN

"How's it going with the dictionary?"

"Making progress!" said Walter. "I've read all the way to *Byzantine*."

On one hand, Ben was impressed. Walter had read thousands of words. On the other hand, he still had several hundred thousand more to go.

"Any new solutions to the riddle?"

"I'm working on a good one," said Walter. "Almost there."

"Great," said Ben. "All that leaves is the birthday question. Any progress?"

Yes. My Great Big Plan now has seven steps.

"Okay," said Ben. "How many steps will it have . . . total?"

"I won't know until I get to the end."

"Are you close?" It was already Wednesday.

"I'm way closer than I was yesterday," said Walter.

Walter has never let me down, Ben reminded himself.

CHAPTER 16

It was time for PE. Ben's class walked down to the gym.

"Today is dodgeball," said Mrs. Bickley.

Ben loved dodgeball. Kyle loved dodgeball. They gave each other a high five. They were the two best dodgeball players in the class, and it wasn't even close.

Mrs. Bickley put Kyle and Ben on different teams.

"Aw, man," said Kyle.

"It wouldn't be fair otherwise," said Ben.

"I know," said Kyle, "but it would be *fun*."

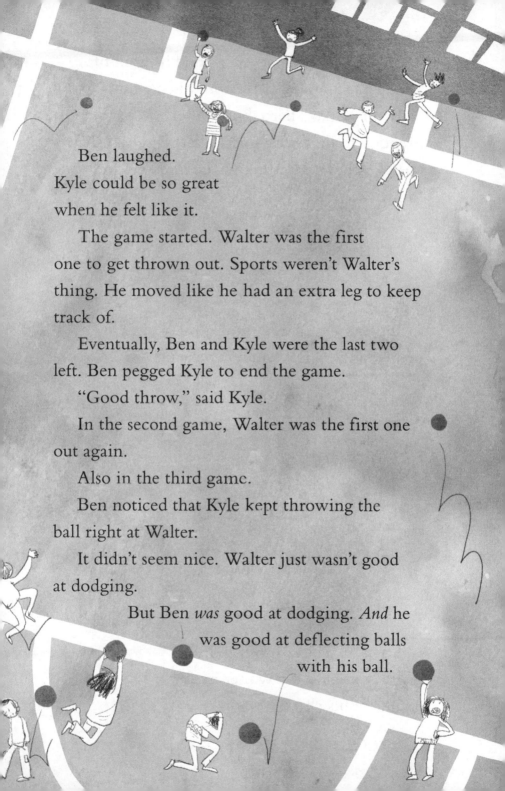

Ben laughed.
Kyle could be so great
when he felt like it.

The game started. Walter was the first
one to get thrown out. Sports weren't Walter's
thing. He moved like he had an extra leg to keep
track of.

Eventually, Ben and Kyle were the last two
left. Ben pegged Kyle to end the game.

"Good throw," said Kyle.

In the second game, Walter was the first one
out again.

Also in the third game.

Ben noticed that Kyle kept throwing the
ball right at Walter.

It didn't seem nice. Walter just wasn't good
at dodging.

But Ben *was* good at dodging. *And* he
was good at deflecting balls
with his ball.

In the fourth game, Ben stood in front of
Walter and kept the balls from hitting him.

Ben felt like a hero, but Walter was paying no
attention to the balls flying all around him. It
was like he was standing in the middle of an
empty room.

Ben kept blocking Kyle's throws anyway.

"Cut it out," said Kyle.

"You cut it out," said Ben. "Throw the ball at
someone else."

Instead, Kyle threw the ball at Walter
again, and Ben just barely blocked it.

Ben!

said Walter.

I figured it out.

What?

said Ben, blocking another throw
that would have hit Walter in the
middle of his chest.

"The answer to the riddle."

"Great. What is it?" Ben leaned as close to Walter as he could while still blocking the balls that Kyle kept throwing at him. "*Quietly*, remember!"

A newborn baby fart.

"*What?!*"

Ben blocked a shot that would have hit Walter in the leg.

"Think about it. A newborn baby fart never existed in the past because the baby hadn't been born until just now."

Ben blocked a shot that would have hit Walter in the shoulder.

"You can't have it today because you can't pick up a fart."

Ben blocked a shot that would have hit Walter in the foot.

"And it disappears the moment it arrives because *that's what farts do*!"

Ben laughed. He laughed hard. He couldn't stop laughing.

Ben remembered. Every once in a while, Walter said something so funny and unexpected that Ben laughed and laughed and couldn't stop.

"I guess you could try to pick it up with the inside of your nose," said Walter.

That made Ben laugh so hard he bent over.

Kyle pegged Walter right in the head.

Walter collapsed like a house of cards that just got hit by a watermelon.

Walter!

Ben suddenly stopped laughing.

Mrs. Bickley came over. "Are you all right, Stillman?"

"I'm okay," said Walter. He sat up, looking woozy.

"Take him to the bleachers, Yokoyama."

As Ben led Walter to the bleachers, he heard Janet giving Kyle a talking-to.

He wasn't even looking!

We're playing dodgeball!

You hit him in the head!

I was aiming for his leg.

I guess I missed.

Ben knew Kyle never missed. Ben helped Walter sit down.

"Are you all right?" Walter didn't look all right.

"Yeah," said Walter, forcing a smile. "I guess I'm bad at dodgeball."

"Dodgeball is dumb," said Ben. In that moment, he meant it.

"I thought you *loved* dodgeball."

Ben *did* love dodgeball. But he didn't love how dodgeball made some people feel bad.

He changed the subject.

Your riddle answer is perfect. A baby's fart, oh man.

Ben was laughing all over again.

Do you think it's right?

Walter perked up a little.

Probably not. But *maybe*.

Walter looked a little disappointed.

Principal Hogan came in and joined the team Ben had been on. He seemed to like playing sports with third graders way more than he liked doing regular principal things.

"I forgot to tell you," said Ben. "Principal Hogan went to Honeycutt."

"He did?"

"Yeah, he was the same grade as my aunt."

They sat there for a second, watching the dodgeball. Principal Hogan was good at dodging and at throwing people out.

"Maybe I'll be the principal someday," said Walter.

Ben wasn't sure about that. Principal Hogan was good at being a principal because he always knew what to say and what to do. Walter never knew what to say or what to do. People always listened to Principal Hogan and followed his lead. He couldn't imagine anyone listening to Walter.

Ben wondered what Walter would be when he grew up. Everything seemed so difficult for him.

"I bet you'd be a great principal," said Ben.

Walter glowed like the morning sky right after the sun comes up.

They kept watching. Soon everyone was out except Principal Hogan and Kyle.

"I still don't know why you answered 'ten' for question number three," said Walter.

It took Ben a second to figure out that Walter was talking about the scavenger hunt.

"Five plus five equals ten," said Ben. "I thought we agreed."

"I agree that five plus five equals ten, but ten isn't the answer to that question." Walter seemed so sure.

"What do you mean?"

"Think about it. There are five sisters. Each sister has one brother."

"Right. That's why there are five brothers!"

"I don't think so," said Walter. "Since they are sisters, the brother each one of them has is just one person. Five sisters. One brother. They all share him."

It was like Ben had gone to bed on earth but woke up on the moon.

Walter was right!

"Why didn't you tell me before?"

Walter paused. "I didn't want to make you mad."

Ben wondered if he would have been mad. He couldn't say for sure.

"Why are you telling me now?"

"Because now I know you're my friend again."

Ben looked around to see if anyone had heard. Then he felt bad for looking around.

Walter *was* his friend. Again.

Ben wanted to say, *Of course you're my friend!*

Instead, he said, "Good job figuring out the right answer."

"Thanks," said Walter, like someone who is waiting for someone else to finish their sentence.

Gym was over. Mrs. Bickley took the dodgeball.

Ben looked over at Janet, who was glaring at Kyle and pointing at Walter.

Kyle dragged his feet all the way to the bleachers.

Sorry, Walter,

he said.

That's okay, said Walter.

It's just a game, right?

Right,

said Kyle.

Ben wanted to walk back to class with Janet and Kyle. But he thought he should probably walk back with Walter.

He ended up walking back alone.

CHAPTER 17

It was Thursday morning. Ben was waiting on the corner. It was extremely cold. Janet was extremely late.

For once, it wasn't raining. But it wasn't snowing, either.

Janet showed up. She was out of breath from rushing.

"Sorry," she said.

"It's okay," said Ben. And he meant it.

They walked along together.

How many answers do you and Kyle have now?

Ben asked.

Three.

How about you and Walter?

Three also.

142

It wasn't true. They only had two. But Ben didn't want to admit it.

It felt awful lying to Janet. Awful like a bad dream or throat so sore it hurts to swallow.

Ben needed to set things right by figuring out a third answer as quickly as he could. And he knew just how to do it.

When they got to school, Ben looked for Principal Hogan, who was outside shooting baskets with the fifth graders.

Ben got right to the point.

"Are you ready to tell me your middle name? I've been waiting patiently."

Principal Hogan looked at Ben like a frying pan looks at an egg.

No, Ben, I am not ready.

Principal Hogan shot the ball, and it swooshed through the basket. The fifth graders cheered. Principal Hogan took a few steps back.

I am not ready now, I will not be ready this afternoon, and I will not be ready next July. The head of the school board does not know my middle name, Ben. My children do not know my middle name.

Principal Hogan shot the ball again. He made another basket. The fifth graders cheered even louder this time. He took a few more steps back.

I like you, Ben. I like you a lot. But you are never, and I mean *never*, going to find out what my middle name is.

Ben thought about that. The fortune had a different opinion.

"I hate to argue," said Ben, "but I am going to find out."

He said it

politely but with no hesitation.

Principal Hogan took a few more steps back. He shot the basketball, and again it went through the hoop. The fifth graders went bananas.

Principal Hogan turned to Ben.

"You seem pretty certain. Should we . . . make a bet?"

Principal Hogan had bet Diggsie Gulpert that a pound of marbles was not heavier than a pound of feathers. He had bet Avie Proffitt that tapirs were not just tiny elephants with their trunks chopped off. Principal Hogan made bets all the time.

Ben had never heard of him losing one.

But there was a first time for everything.

Sure.

What's the bet?

Principal Hogan looked at Ben like a microscope looks at a plate of bacteria.

How about this? If you don't find out my middle name by the end of the week, you'll have to scrape all the gum off the gum pole.

Ben shuddered. Right outside the school was a pole that everyone stuck their gum to before going inside.

It was a sticky, speckly, spectacular mess. Every once in a while, someone scraped all the gum off so that the gum pole could start all over again. Ben did not want to be that someone.

But, according to the fortune, he wouldn't have to be.

"All right," said Ben. "And what do I get when I *do* find out your name?"

Principal Hogan gave Ben a look like an ocean gives a raindrop.

"How about ten extra minutes of recess for third grade on Friday?"

"For third *and* fourth grade!" said Ben. He was feeling bold.

"Why don't we just go ahead and make it the whole school?" said Principal Hogan in the casual way someone might have said, *Please hand me a tissue. I have to blow my nose.*

He shot the basketball again. It arced high through the air but bounced off the rim. The fifth graders were devastated.

Principal Hogan gave Ben a wink.

You can't win them all,

he said.

Speak for yourself, thought Ben.

CHAPTER 18

At partner time,
Walter had a jumbo-
size smile on his face.

Ben was in no
mood for goofing.
Kyle and Janet had
three points already.
He and Walter
needed a third
answer in order to
catch up. *And* so that
Ben could get rid of
the awful knot in his
stomach.

Walter kept smiling. It
made Ben mad.

"What?" Ben demanded.

But what he meant was *Stop goofing so we can get down to business.*

Walter didn't get the message. "I found it!" He was wound up and already loud.

"Found what?" Ben put his hand on Walter's arm to try to calm him down.

"One of the words with all five vowels in alphabetical order. *I found it!*"

"Great!" said Ben. If it was true, then both of Ben's problems were solved. But only if it was true.

"What is it? *Quietly!*"

Ben whispered to remind Walter what "quietly" meant.

Walter calmed down and got serious. He
leaned in and whispered,

Abstemious.

And then he looked at
Ben like an empty shelf
that's waiting for a trophy.

Ben had never heard the word before
and wondered if Walter was making it up.
"Write it down," he said.
Walter did.

Abstemious

Ben took a close look. There were all five
vowels! In alphabetical order! *Walter had actually
done it!*

"Are you sure it's an actual word?"

"It is!"

"What does it mean?"

"I'm not completely sure. The definition was made up of words I didn't know the definitions of, either!"

But it didn't matter. The scavenger hunt just said to find the word. It hadn't said anything about needing to know what it meant.

Ben's aching heart sighed with relief.

WHEW!

"I can't believe you found it!" Ben was being a little loud himself. "Great job!"

Ben's smile was like catnip to Walter.

"I found it on Tuesday. It was right at the beginning of the alphabet."

This made Ben mad.

On *Tuesday*! Why didn't you tell me before?

Ben's words
knocked Walter
right off his perch.

"I wanted it to be a surprise."

"No surprises!" said Ben. "We're partners. I need to know all the facts!"

Ben didn't even know what he meant by that. On one hand, he was glad that they had caught up with Janet and Kyle. But on the other hand, it actually *had* been true when he'd told Janet they had three points. If he'd known that Walter had found the word, he wouldn't have had to lie about it.

Sorry, Ben.

Walter looked sad and a little bit lost.

Ben saw that Walter was sorry, but he didn't want to forgive him. Not yet. He was looking for a reason to act as mad as he felt.

152

Why do you still have the dictionary?

Mr. P. said there were two words with all the vowels in alphabetical order. I want to find the other one.

Ben found his reason. "We don't *need* to find the other one! One is enough!"

"But I want to find it," said Walter. "If I don't find it, I'll keep wondering what it is."

Ben was furious now. Walter was missing the point.

"We don't have time to find unnecessary words," said Ben. "We have to solve the riddle. And figure out which three kids have the same birthday. Why don't you focus on that?"

Walter looked at Ben like someone who thought he was playing chess and then found out it was actually dodgeball.

Ben knew he was being unkind and unfair, but he didn't know how to fix it. He didn't know what to say. He didn't want to sit there waiting to feel better. He wanted to *do* something instead.

He took out their answer sheet so he could write down the answer to question number two.

"What was that word again?" he asked, trying his hardest to be patient and kind.

"What word?"

The word with all the vowels in alphabetical order! *The word we've been talking about this whole time!*

154

"Abstemious!" said Walter so loudly that people might have heard it on the far side of Saturn.

Every head in the room turned to look at Walter. Every team now had the answer to the second question.

"Ugh!" It was Ben's turn to be loud. He glared at Walter like the moment before a bolt of lightning strikes. "Why are you always such a . . . ?"

Ben stopped himself just in time.

Walter looked like a window that just got hit by a rock.

Such a what?

"Nothing," said Ben, closing his notebook and stomping back to his own desk. Everyone was watching. Ben wanted them to stop.

What were you going to say?

asked Walter again, shouting across the classroom.

Tell me!

Ben wouldn't answer. He couldn't look at Walter. He didn't want to say what he was thinking. He wanted Walter to go away.

SUCH A WHAT, BEN?

Walter was yelling now. Walter was crying.

WHY WON'T YOU SAY IT?

Come on, Walter,
let's take a walk,

said Mr. P.

As he led Walter to the door, Mr. P. gave Ben a look that he would never forget. It was the look you give someone you always thought was one kind of person but then found out was something else entirely.

Ben wanted to be this first kind of person. He didn't even know who the other Ben was.

He could hear Walter sobbing in the hallway.

"You should have just said it," said Kyle. "Somebody needs to."

"Shut up, Kyle," said Ben.

"What's wrong with you?" asked Kyle.

"I wish I knew," said Ben.

CHAPTER 19

After lunch, Walter was back. He seemed okay.
He didn't look at Ben.

They were doing multiplication drills, but
Walter spent the whole time writing in his
notebook and not paying attention. Mr. P. didn't
give him a hard time about it.

The bell rang and school was over.

Walter walked over to Ben and handed him a
note. "Here," he said.

Ben wanted to say he was sorry. He wanted to
give Walter a hug.

Instead, he said,

What's this?

But Walter walked away without answering.

Ben opened the note. This is what it said:

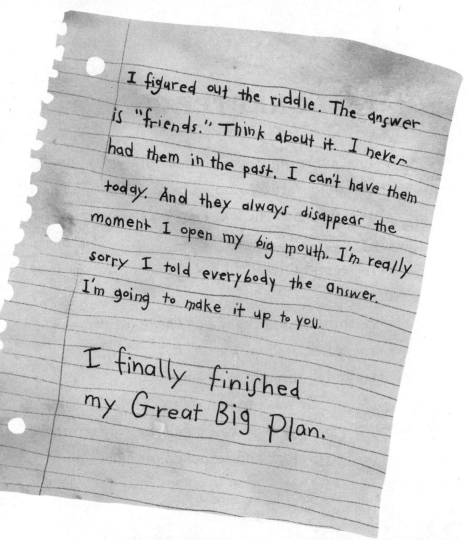

I figured out the riddle. The answer is "friends." Think about it. I never had them in the past. I can't have them today. And they always disappear the moment I open my big mouth. I'm really sorry I told everybody the answer. I'm going to make it up to you.

I finally finished my Great Big Plan.

Ben thought about that.

Walter had never let him down before.

Ben wished that he could say the same.

CHAPTER 20

The next morning it was cold *and* snowy, so school would start two hours late.

Ben's first thought was *I don't have to rake leaves today!*

His second thought was *I can finally use my new sled!*

His third thought was *But I don't feel like using my new sled.*

His fourth thought was *Janet.*

It was too snowy to climb the oak tree, so Ben walked all the way around the block and knocked on Janet's door.

Can I come in?

Sure. Do you want to talk about it?

Ben didn't.

"Do you want to play cribbage?"

Ben did.

Cribbage was an extremely strange card game with extremely complicated rules that Ben had finally learned how to play but was still really bad at.

Janet beat Ben every time. It wasn't a matter of whether Ben would lose but whether he would get *skunked,* which was the official cribbage term for losing so soundly that cribbage wanted you to feel terrible about it.

Ben's dad told him that losing constantly at cribbage was good for his character. Ben's mom told him that he just needed to practice more. His dad liked playing games just to play them, but his mom liked winning.

Ben liked winning, too.

It was Ben's turn to count his hand. He had a four, an ace, and a pair of twos. The pair was worth two points, which was almost as bad as a cribbage hand could be.

"Tough luck," said Janet, hiding a smile that worried Ben.

It was her turn to count. She had a jack and four fives, which is what cribbage gives your opponent when it's trying to make you actually cry.

"Twenty-nine points," said Janet. "Yikes!" she said, trying hard to seem sorry while swimming in an ocean of glee.

Janet moved her peg halfway around the board.

Usually, it would have hurt. But today, losing to Janet at cribbage was helping Ben keep his mind off the Great Big Thing that hurt even worse.

Ben shuffled the cards. It was his turn to deal.

"I know it's hard," said Janet.

"The fact that I'm going to get skunked again?"

Janet laughed. "Yes, that, but also being Walter's partner."

"Yeah," said Ben.

"I get the sense he can't help himself when he does things like that."

"Yeah," said Ben again. He couldn't imagine how hard it must be to be Walter.

Janet's words helped Ben open a window that had been stuck. Suddenly some breeze came in.

I still like him,

said Ben.

It felt important to say it to himself and admit it to Janet.

"I get that," said Janet. "He's very likable. Except when he's shouting out the answers to scavenger-hunt questions."

"Exactly!" said Ben. It meant everything that Janet understood. "I want to be his friend, but if it's always going to be this hard, I'm not sure I can."

Janet put down her cards and looked Ben in the eye.

"I had a friend named Dot. She was smart and funny and creative, and we did everything together."

"She sounds great," said Ben. He was a little jealous.

She *was* great.

Janet leaned into the word "was" like she was pushing a piano off a cliff.

"But not anymore?"

Instead of answering Ben's question, Janet marched on with her story.

"One day in first
grade, a girl named
Tiffany Jorgenson moved to town. Tiffany
Jorgenson had purple nail polish and a pet
chinchilla. Suddenly Dot stopped being
interested in me and became the world's number
one fan of Tiffany Jorgenson."

"Why couldn't all three of you be friends?"

"Tiffany said I was boring."

Ben was outraged. *"You are not boring!"*

"Thanks," said Janet like she needed to hear it.

"What happened?" Ben was desperate to know.
There was no better friend than Janet. She was
smart. She was funny. She was kind and generous
and honest and knew what she believed in.

If Janet could lose her best friend, then it could
happen to anybody! *It could happen to him!*

"Nothing happened, really. One day Dot was my friend, and the next day she wasn't. I ate lunch by myself for a while."

"That's awful!" said Ben, who couldn't imagine anything worse than Janet sitting by herself at lunch. "What did you *do*?"

"I didn't *do* anything. I was just miserable. Eventually, the school year ended, and Mom and I moved here. Eventually, things got better."

Ben thought about that. Janet was wrong. She hadn't done *nothing*. She had done *something* extremely wise.

"You *waited*," he said.

Janet weighed her thoughts as if they were bananas and she wanted to know how much they were going to cost before she decided to buy them.

"I guess I did," she said, her spirits lifting like
a leaf does when the sun comes out. "I waited
and waited, and one day . . . a really good thing
finally happened."

"What was it?" Ben needed to know.

"*You,* silly," said Janet. "You were the good
thing that waiting brought to me. You are the
good thing that came."

Ben's heart felt huge. But the rest of him was
still as mad as fists.

"I'd like to give Dot a piece of my mind."

"I already did," said Janet. "After we moved, I
wrote her a letter telling her exactly how bad
she'd made me feel."

"And what did she say?"

"I never heard back."

"That stinks."

It wasn't what Ben wanted to hear. He needed to know exactly what had gone wrong so that he could keep it from happening to Janet and him. And Dot was the only one who had the answers.

"Maybe you could call her?"

"Ben, I'm over it. Really."

"But—"

"Really," said Janet like a dead bolt sliding into place.

"But don't you want to know what . . . happened?"

"I don't think so. Why does it matter? I'm just lucky I found a new friend named Ben, who is willing to play cribbage with me even though I beat him every time."

Janet's joke helped Ben calm down.

He sounds like a pretty good guy.

He's all right.

Ben was talking to Janet, but he was thinking about Walter.

When Janet had lost Dot, she'd found Ben.

When Walter had lost Ben . . . he'd become the kid that always gets picked last for partner projects.

Walter needed a Ben.

Fortunately, Ben knew where he could find one.

"It doesn't mean you have to be Walter's best friend," said Janet, reading Ben's thoughts like they were printed on a billboard. "You already have one of those. But you can be the kind of friend who stands up for him when some jerk throws dodgeballs at his head."

"Yeah," said Ben, feeling glad he had done it but wishing he'd done a lot more.

"And I can help, too," said Janet. "Being friends with Walter might work best as a group effort."

"That sounds like a really good plan," said Ben, amazed that of all the people Janet could have chosen as her best friend, she had picked him.

Janet gave Ben a look like a razor gives a full bushy beard.

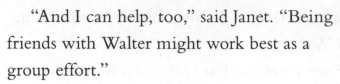

Ready to play?

Ben picked up his cards.

Ready.

He lost the next three
games but almost
won the fourth.
Almost.

CHAPTER 21

When it was finally time for school, Janet and Ben took turns pulling each other along the sidewalk on Ben's sled.

While Ben pulled, he thought about Walter. He knew he had to set things right. By the time he got to school, he had a plan.

Walter would look over at him like Walter always did. Ben would give Walter a smile, and Walter would know that Ben was still his friend. That he was sorry for what had happened. And that everything was going to be okay. They wouldn't even have to talk about it.

But for the first time ever, Walter didn't look. He was staring at a piece of paper like a pirate stares at a treasure map.

Ben figured he'd try the plan again at lunch.

Because of the snow delay, lunch started twenty minutes after they got to school.

Ben sat with Kyle and Lang. Janet sat with Emma and Kamari.

Walter sat with . . .

Ben looked around. Walter wasn't there.

EXCUSE ME, PLEASE.

Someone was shouting in a voice you could have heard in the next galaxy.

Everyone stopped talking at once.

The room fell as silent as a snowy night.

Every eyeball turned toward the far end of the cafeteria and locked into place. There was Walter, standing on the stage, all by himself.

The stage was for assemblies and presentations and teachers reminding students when permission slips were due. It was not for third graders doing whatever it was that Walter was doing.

What is Walter doing? Ben wondered.

EXCUSE ME!!

Walter thundered like a summer storm.

I NEED TO KNOW WHICH THREE PEOPLE IN THIS ROOM HAVE THE SAME BIRTHDAY. DOES ANYONE KNOW?

No one said a word. Everyone was shocked and silent, as if an alien had just slithered out of the milk machine.

That was step one of the Great Big Plan.

Since no one knows, we'll move on to step two, which is to divide into smaller groups.

Ben saw what Walter was suggesting. It *was* a good idea. Sometimes when a problem was too big to tackle all at once, you had to break it into smaller problems.

It might work! *If* everyone went along with it.

There had never been a bigger *if* in the history of Honeycutt Elementary.

Silence gave way to whispers as the initial shock wore off, and kids started asking each other what was going on. But Walter didn't seem to notice as the Great Big Plan continued.

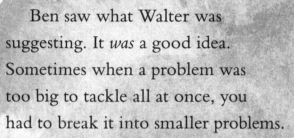

If everyone with birthdays from January to June would please meet at that corner of the cafeteria.

Walter pointed to the corner with
the milk machine.

And if everyone with
birthdays from July
to December would go
into that corner . . .

Ben couldn't believe it. Even
though no one was helping him
at all, Walter just kept steaming
forward, like a ship that hits
iceberg after iceberg but
refuses to sink.

Ben liked ships like that.

Ben knew that he could watch and wait and
that nothing bad would happen to *him*. But he also
knew that every second he waited would make
things worse for Walter. People were starting to
snicker. And make jokes. Walter was such an easy
target. Ben knew that if he waited much longer,
everyone would start laughing and Walter would
run into the iceberg that might finally sink him.

Ben took out his fortune.

Good things come to those who wait.

Sorry, Fortune, thought Ben.

He stood up and walked toward the stage.

"Hey, everybody," said Ben.

All at once, every eyeball peeled itself away from Walter and locked onto Ben instead. "Walter hasn't told you the most exciting part of his Great Big Plan."

Ben had everyone's attention. People liked exciting things.

He walked up the steps and stood on the stage.

"First of all, Walter has a really good idea."

Walter smiled. He suddenly stood taller, like a timid giraffe who just figured out how his neck works.

"But we're going to need everyone's help to pull it off."

Ben looked out and saw Flegg McEggers, a fifth grader who loved nothing more than picking on anyone who was smaller than he was.

Flegg was gnawing on his sandwich as if it were Ben's foot.

So far, this isn't exciting,

said Flegg.

"Thanks for the reminder, Flegg," said Ben. "We know you're all busy eating lunch, so we wouldn't ask for your help without *offering you something* in return."

Everyone leaned in. People liked getting something in return.

"If you help Walter and me answer our question, Principal Hogan will give everyone ten extra minutes of recess today."

A buzz of delirious excitement spread throughout the cafeteria.

"You can't promise that," said Flegg.

"I can." Being onstage made Ben feel bold. "I just did."

Flegg didn't like Ben's attitude, but Ben didn't care. He looked at the clock. Lunch would be over in ten minutes. They had to get started right away.

"This is outrageous," said Amy Lou Bonnerman. "We have too much recess already!"

The thunder of boos made it clear that no one shared Amy Lou's opinion.

But she was not discouraged. "I am here to learn."

"I'll do multiplication drills with you during the extra recess," said Janet. "You'll learn even more than you would in math class."

"That would be appreciated," said Amy Lou, who didn't seem entirely satisfied.

Ben shot Janet a look of thanks.

Janet gave Ben a double thumbs-up.

"So," said Ben, "will you help us?"

"Yeah," said about half of the kids, with about as much excitement as a clump of seaweed at low tide.

"Sorry, but we are going to need *everyone's* help to make this work. *Will you help us for the sake of extra recess?*"

"*Yeah!*" said everyone with the excitement of a two-hundred-piece marching band playing recently polished trombones.

Everyone but Flegg, who scowled like a brontosaurus who just stepped on a triceratops.

"All right," said Ben, "we don't have much time. It would help if we could break into four groups instead of two. Which means we need two more group leaders."

"I'll help!" It was Janet.

"What are you doing?" said Kyle. "They're the *competition*."

"They're my *friends*," said Janet. "We could use *your* help, too, Kyle. You might kind of *owe it* to Walter to pitch in."

Kyle scowled. "Fine," he said, "but if the people with the same birthdays are in Janet's group or my group, then *we* get the points for the scavenger hunt."

Fine,

said Ben.

He wasn't even thinking about the scavenger hunt. He felt like he was piloting a broken helicopter, and all he really wanted was to land without crashing.

Fine!

said Janet.

She was clearly mad at Kyle, which made Ben secretly happy.

"Great!" said Walter. He was extremely excited. His Great Big Plan was actually happening.

A few minutes later, there were groups of kids in each corner of the cafeteria.

Janet had January through March.

Kyle had April through June.

Walter had July through September.

Ben had October through December.

The Acadio twins were in his group! That had to be a good sign. Now that the helicopter was closer to the ground, he was starting to care about the scavenger hunt again.

He started with October 1 and marched through the calendar, reading off each date and asking people to raise their hands when he called out their birthday.

October came and went, so Ben launched into November.

November nineteenth, said Ben.

November twentieth.

November twenty-first.

The Acadio twins raised their hands. But no one else did.

Ben tried not to be disappointed. There was still some of November and all of December to go. He kept calling out the dates, but as he neared the end of December, his hopes began to dwindle.

December thirty-first.

No one raised a hand.

Okay. Thanks, everyone. The three people with the same birthday aren't in our group.

Ben looked around. Janet and Kyle were already done, and Walter seemed to be finishing up. He couldn't tell which of them had found the three birthdays.

But we still get extra recess,

said Flegg, standing way too close to Ben's face. It wasn't a question.

Of course.

But as the words tumbled out of Ben's mouth, he remembered something extremely important. He hadn't *officially* won the bet yet.

Ben blamed the fortune.

But the fortune wasn't the one that Flegg was going to pummel if Ben didn't keep his promise.

He needed to find out Principal Hogan's middle name. And he needed to find out *now*.

CHAPTER 22

Ben found Walter on the far side of the cafeteria. They looked at each other for a second and then spoke at the very same time.

They both laughed and both spoke at the same time again.

"I didn't have any luck with the birthdays," said Ben. "How about you?"

"They weren't in my group, either," said Walter.

Ben's heart grew as heavy as a full bag of cans. The three students with the same birthday were either in Janet's group or Kyle's.

Walter's Great Big Plan had actually worked, but someone else was going to get the points. It wasn't fair.

But there wasn't time to dwell on it. Ben had a Flegg-flavored problem to solve.

Ben looked Walter in the eye. He placed his hands on Walter's shoulders. "We need to figure out Principal Hogan's middle name right away."

"Great news," said Walter, pointing across the room. "He's right over there."

Ben looked. Principal Hogan was standing at the far end of the cafeteria, talking to Amy Lou Bonnerman. It was clear from her expression that she was sharing her concerns about the dangers of too much recess.

Principal Hogan had on his *I am confused* face. But as Amy Lou kept talking, it turned into his *And now I am extremely irritated* face. And then suddenly it exploded into his *And where is Ben Yokoyama at this very moment?* face.

"Principal Hogan!" Walter shrieked, waving both of his hands.

Ben's heart nearly stopped as Principal Hogan's head turned to find out who had shouted his name. Ben yanked Walter down behind a lunch table just in time.

What are you doing?

Walter looked a little confused but also a lot excited. He could tell that something dramatic was happening.

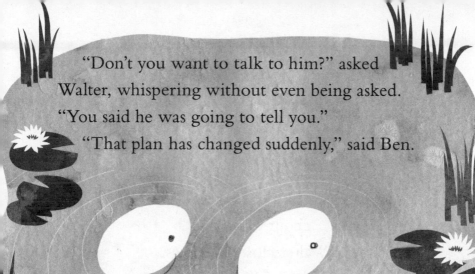

"Don't you want to talk to him?" asked
Walter, whispering without even being asked.
"You said he was going to tell you."

"That plan has changed suddenly," said Ben.

Walter's eyes grew wide like the
rings when you toss a pebble in a pond.

"Are you saying we need . . . a new plan?"

"That's exactly what I'm saying."

"Does it need to be . . . ?"

Walter was so excited that he couldn't finish
his sentence. So Ben did it for him.

"Yes, this plan needs to be Great and Big."

Walter looked like a too-full balloon that's
just about to pop.

"And *Fast,*" Ben added, knowing that Walter's
Great Big Plans were often the opposite.

"Got it, Ben," said Walter. "No problem."

Walter
was a
rocket rumbling on
the launching pad.
His engines were
firing. He was
about to take off.
Walter closed his eyes.
Ben held his breath.
Principal Hogan was
scanning the lunchroom, looking
for Honeycutt's Most Wanted.
Ben was scared but also excited.
In that moment, he remembered every
adventure that he and Walter had ever
taken and every Great Big Plan they'd ever
made. They had gotten themselves in
trouble plenty of times, but somehow
they'd always managed to get themselves
back out.

In that moment, Ben understood Walter
perfectly. Some things were just too interesting
and exciting to be quiet about.

Ben surprised himself by reaching out and grabbing Walter's hand and giving it a squeeze. He almost looked around to see if anyone had noticed, but then he decided that he didn't care.

Walter smiled and squeezed back, and then his eyes flew open like cannonballs firing. "I've got it!"

Ben's heart shot into the sky like a backward asteroid. "You've got it?"

"I've got it!" Walter shrieked.

It is Great! It is BIG!

And Superfast!

Walter beamed. He was proud.

"Tell me the plan!" said Ben, who was still shooting through space and needed to know where they were going to land.

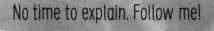

No time to explain. Follow me!

Walter was on a roller coaster, and Ben decided to go along for the ride.

Using a fifth grader named Damascus as a human shield, they slipped out of the cafeteria.

Walter raced down the hall, and Ben raced with him.

"How old is your aunt?" asked Walter as they jogged.

"Forty-four. Why?"

But Walter didn't explain. "That would mean she was in fifth grade . . . thirty-three years ago."

Ben glanced back down the hallway behind them. There was Principal Hogan, looking as mad as a clam with a cramp, and still searching for something named Ben.

"In here," said Walter, taking a sharp turn into—

"The library?" Ben asked. He didn't understand.

"No time to explain," said Walter as he marched right up to the circulation desk.

Hello, Walter,

said Mrs. Piendak.

What are you looking for today?

The Honeycutt yearbook from 1988, please!

Mrs. Piendak smiled the smile of someone who has just been completely surprised and is enjoying how it feels.

"I think we have a box of old yearbooks in the back."

Principal Hogan stormed down the hallway and right past the library door. He hadn't seen Ben. *Yet.* It was only a matter of time.

"As quickly as possible, please," said Ben.

Mrs. Piendak frowned the frown of someone who has just been asked to hurry and doesn't like it one bit. "Patience is a virtue, young man."

"Yes, ma'am," said Ben with his *Under most circumstances, I would agree with you* face.

Mrs. Piendak gave a "Hrumph" that would have made Ben's mom proud and headed into the back room.

Ben hid behind the library counter.

Tell me when she comes back.

Maybe eighteen seconds passed.

SHE'S BACK!!

said Walter in a voice that could probably be heard in a different dimension.

Here you go,

said Mrs. Piendak, handing the yearbook to Walter.

Here you go,

said Walter,

handing it to Ben.

I don't understand,

said Ben, who hated not understanding.

This is from the year your aunt and Principal Hogan were both in fifth grade,

Walter explained.

Their names should be inside. Hopefully, their *full* names.

Walter, you're a genius!

Walter got the look of someone who had just learned to fly and was about to jump out of the nest.

No other kid in the school would have come up with the plan. No one else *could* have. Not only was it Great, Big, and Superfast, it had also *worked*.

Ben took the yearbook and thumbed through to the *H*'s.

And there he was, an eleven-year-old Principal Hogan, with a full head of hair and funny old glasses. Right beneath his picture was his name. His *full* name.

Reading Principal Hogan's middle name was like watching twelve clowns try to ride on one unicycle while juggling actual chickens.

It was the most ridiculous middle name in the history of time. If there had been a contest for ridiculous names, the name would have won first, second, *and* third place.

Oh wow, said Ben.

Oh man. Can you believe it?

Ben looked over at Walter. He wouldn't be able to fully enjoy the thrilling spectacle of Principal Hogan's middle name until he could share it with somebody else.

But Walter had his hands over his eyes.

It's better if I don't know what it is. That way I can't mess it up.

Ben felt bad. "I trust you," he said.

"You shouldn't," said Walter.

"Listen," said Ben. "We might not win this scavenger hunt, but you're the only reason we have as many answers as we do."

Walter peeked out from behind his hands.

"*You're* the one who figured out the brothers question. *You're* the one who found the word with all the vowels. *You're* the one who came up with a solution to the birthday problem. And now *you're* the one who figured out Principal Hogan's middle name. I think you deserve to know how ridiculous it is."

Walter thought about that. "I guess you're right!"

Walter's smile popped above the surface of his sadness like a great ship un-sinking from the sea.

"Okay," he said with an excited grin. "I'll look."

Walter looked. His eyes grew wide. He made a smile that would have melted a glacier the size of the moon.

Ben and Walter looked at each other and laughed louder and longer than they ever had before. It was even better than a baby fart.

What are you two giggling about?

asked Mrs. Piendak.

Let me see!

But just then something thundered into the library looking as mad as a smashed trash can. It was Principal Hogan.

"What's this about you promising everyone ten extra minutes of recess, Ben?"

"It was less of a promise and more of a guarantee," Ben clarified. Halfway through his sentence, he realized that it probably wasn't the best moment for a vocabulary lesson.

"You must not understand how bets work, Ben," said Principal Hogan with a face that was mad, smug, and amused all at once. "To win the extra recess, you have to actually *know* my middle name. I think it's time for you to step out front and say hello to the gum pole, because no matter how hard you try, no matter how long you wait, you will *never*—"

That's when Principal Hogan
noticed the yearbook.

Ben handed it to him as if it
were an extremely hot spoon.

Principal Hogan took it as if it
were an extremely aggressive lobster.

He flipped through the yearbook until he
found the page with the *H*'s. Then
he took a deep, deep breath.

"Gentlemen, I am
impressed. You have
accomplished the impossible.
However, I must request
that you not share this
information. Not ever. Not
with anyone. Not even your
parakeet."

Ben did not have a parakeet.

"But it's the answer to one of
the clues on the scavenger
hunt!" said Walter.

"I am aware of this
unfortunate fact," said
Principal Hogan.

"Two wrongs don't make a right," said Ben.

"Those are wise words indeed," said Principal Hogan. "But I wonder if two . . . fifteen-minute stretches of extra recess might make a right under the present circumstances."

"So thirty minutes total?" asked Walter.

"Your math is sound, young man," said Principal Hogan.

"For the third grade?" asked Ben.

"For the whole school," said Principal Hogan with a grateful smile.

Ben thought about it. He knew how much Flegg would appreciate an extra half hour of recess. And how much Amy Lou Bonnerman would hate it.

"I think we have a deal," he said.

Ben was glad to have won the bet. But he was disappointed that they'd missed yet another opportunity to score points for the scavenger hunt.

Principal Hogan put on his *We're almost done but not quite done* face. "Who else knows my middle name?"

"Just me and Walter," said Ben.

"And you two promise to keep it to yourselves?" said Principal Hogan, giving Walter a look like a flamethrower gives a pile of greasy rags.

GULP

Or else I'll swallow an ostrich,

said Walter, placing his hand over his heart.

Principal Hogan made a face like he'd really like to see that. But then he made his principal face again and looked right at Mrs. Piendak.

"I would like to check out this yearbook forever. If you need it, it will be locked in the safe in my office."

"But I don't have the combination to your safe!" said Mrs. Piendak.

"Exactly," said Principal Hogan. "And you two had better get back to your classroom."

Ben remembered. *It was time for the scavenger-hunt tally!*

"Let's go," he said to Walter.

"And, Ben—" Principal Hogan had on his *I may be forever in your debt, but don't forget* I'm *still the principal* face.

"Yes?"

Next time, wait until you've actually won a bet to claim your prize.

Good advice,

said Ben.

But Ben's brain wondered if it actually *was* good advice. Once again he *hadn't* waited, and the good thing had happened anyway.

*Was the fortune right or wrong?
Or possibly both?*

CHAPTER 23

Ben and Walter walked back to their classroom.

"Just so you know, that was the greatest Great Big Plan ever," said Ben. "And I'm really sorry we won't get points for it."

"That's okay," said Walter. "I'm just glad we figured out the answer!"

Ben realized something he'd always suspected but never believed could actually be true.

You really *don't* care about winning, do you?

Winning would be nice,

said Walter.

But it's not as fun as all the parts that come before it.

Ben thought about that.

Playing cribbage with Janet was fun even though she beat him every time.

Playing dodgeball was the fun thing.

Winning meant the fun part was over.

Walter was wise. *Except* when it came to solving riddles.

"Just so you know," said Ben, "your most recent guess on the riddle was all wrong."

It took Walter a second to realize that Ben was referring to the note.

"You *did* have a friend in the past," said Ben. "And you *do* have one today. And no matter what you think, I'm not going *anywhere.*"

Ben put his hand on Walter's shoulder.

Walter's eyes were full of tears. For the first time in a long time, he had nothing to say.

"And I'm not going to," Ben continued.

They stood there for a minute, two old friends who suddenly felt new.

Walter got a look like he was hatching yet another Great Big Plan.

"What is it?" Ben was excited. Walter was really on a roll.

"What if the actual answer to the riddle is all the fun things we haven't done yet?"

"What do you mean?"

"Think about it. The things we haven't done yet didn't exist in the past, right?"

Ben's brain gnawed on the question like it was a mouthful of slightly stale marshmallows.

Right.

"And if something hasn't happened yet, that means you can't have it today, right?"

"Right."

"And whatever fun thing hasn't happened yet disappears the moment it arrives, because at that moment, it becomes a fun thing that has already happened."

Ben felt a little dizzy,
but once his brain stopped
spinning, what Walter
was saying made a whole
lot of sense.

Ben could think of one
simple way to describe all
the fun things they hadn't
yet done together.

Ben *knew* it was the answer to the riddle. The
actual answer. The answer that would win them
an actual point.

Ben meant it. They were back in the running for the scavenger hunt!

And whether or not they got the most points, and whatever Mr. P.'s prize turned out to be, Ben suspected they'd already won something better.

CHAPTER 24

When Ben and Walter got back to the classroom, everyone else was already sitting at their desks, excited and waiting and extremely impatient. Mr. P. was standing in the front of the room next to the list of questions.

Welcome, Ben and Walter.

We were about to send out a search party.

"Sorry," said Ben as he walked over to his desk and sat down. "We were just doing a little last-minute research in the library."

"No fair!" said Amy Lou.

"I can think of things that are less fair," said Mr. P., giving Ben a kind smile.

And in
that
moment,
Ben could
tell that he
had been
forgiven,
that Mr. P.
knew that
he was still
the kind
of person
he'd always
been,
and that
everyone
gets lost in
the woods
every now
and then.

"All right," said Mr. P. next. "It's the moment you've all been waiting for. Are you ready to tally the final results?"

"Yes!" said everyone at once, like a gaggle of hungry ducks lunging for the same crust of bread.

"All right, then. Take out your answer sheets," said Mr. P. "First question. What is something that never existed in the past, you can't have today, and disappears the moment it arrives?"

Hands shot up all over the room.

"Yes, Quinten?"

The ghost of an imaginary doughnut.

"Hmm," said Mr. P. "A fascinating guess. But not the answer I was looking for, unfortunately. Who else?"

My grandma's goldfish,

said Devin.

It died the moment we arrived at her condo. It didn't *disappear*, exactly, but . . . you know.

"An excellent guess and a tragic outcome," said Mr. P. "And yet, I'm thinking of a different solution." Mr. P. looked around the room. "Yes . . . Lang?

"The future!" shouted Lang.

"Correct," said Mr. P. with a smile.

And all the other groups agreed.

Ben and Walter exchanged a high five.

After one question, we have a seven-way tie for first place,

said Mr. P., making marks on the board to keep track of the points.

As for question two, what's a word with all five vowels in alphabetical order?

Everyone raised their hands.

"Bob?" said Mr. P.

"Abstema-somethingorother," said Bob.

"Abstemious," said Amy Lou Bonnerman.

"That's right," said Mr. P. "And I think we all owe Walter a big thanks for sharing his hard work on this question with the rest of us."

"Thanks, Walter," said Amy Lou.

"Thanks, Walter," said everyone but Kyle.

"Now . . . does anyone know what this word *means*?" asked Mr. P.

Only Walter raised his hand.

Mr. P. nodded.

Temperate, moderate, self-disciplined, and restrained, said Walter, as if he were reading the ingredients on the side of a cereal box.

"In other words?"

"I think it means someone who can keep his big mouth shut," said Walter.

No one knew if it was okay to laugh. But then Walter laughed, so Ben did, too. And then so did everyone else.

"That's right," said Mr. P., chuckling.

"Since everyone knows the correct answer, for a bonus point, does anyone know the *other* word with five vowels in alphabetical order?"

Ben was mad at himself. He'd told Walter not to look for the other word.

But Walter's hand shot up like the basket end of a catapult.

So did Janet's.

Ben remembered. *Janet had a great vocabulary.*

"Well?" said Mr. P.

"Facetious," said Walter and Janet at the same time.

"Excellent! That's a bonus point for each of your teams. Do you know what it means?"

"It's when you say something that sounds serious but is actually a joke," said Janet.

"Can you give an example?"

"The word 'facetious' is not so easy to spell!' " said Janet.

Mr. P. chuckled.

Great job.

Okay, after two rounds, we have a two-way tie for first place.

Kyle and Janet on one team.

Ben and Walter on the other.

Kyle and Janet gave each other a high five.

"I'm so glad you kept looking for the other word," said Ben. "I'm so sorry I told you not to."

"I couldn't help myself," said Walter, smiling. "I found it this morning at breakfast!"

"All right," said Mr. P. "Question three. Megan has five daughters. Each daughter has one brother. How many children does Megan have?"

"This one was too easy," said Amy Lou Bonnerman.

"How about you tell us the answer, then?" said Mr. P.

"Ten," said Amy Lou.

"Who else thinks the answer is ten?" Mr. P. looked around the room.

About half the students raised their hands. But not Ben or Walter. Not Janet or Kyle. Not Grace or Kamari or Jackson or Lucy T.

"How could you guys have gotten it wrong?" said Amy Lou with a satisfied smirk.

"Were there any *other* answers?" asked Mr. P.

"Six," said Janet. "Five girls, one boy. The sisters all share the same brother."

Wrong! said Amy Lou, like an extremely proud peacock. But then she said, Oh ... right, like an extremely sullen snail.

"We still have a tie for first," said Mr. P. "But it's about to be broken. How about each team sends one member up to the board to write out your palindrome."

Lucy T. wrote, STOP IT, TIPOTS.
Amy Lou wrote, DO NOT BOB TO NOD.
Lucy Q. wrote, EVIL OLIVE.
"That's not ten letters!" said Kyle.
"But still pretty good," said Taevon.
Jackson wrote, wow tuna nut wow.
Lang wrote, A BUTT TUBA.
That got some chuckles.
Bob wrote, BOB sees BOB.
"No fair!" said Malcolm.
"Every time I look in the mirror," said Bob.
Sunil wrote Step on no pets.
And Ben wrote, NOT NOW, WONTON.
It got a few chuckles, but not as many as Ben had hoped for.
"Anyone else?" said Mr. P.

Janet stood up and walked
to the board and wrote,

MR. OWL ATE MY METAL WORM.

At first, no one said anything. Janet's
palindrome was just that spectacular. And then
the class started cheering and clapping. Janet gave
a little bow.

"I'm impressed," said Mr. P. "With *all* of you.
Palindromes are tricky. I'm tempted to give each
of you a point, but . . . we need to break this tie."

Mr. P. read each of the palindromes one by
one, asking the class to clap for the ones they
liked best.

A BUTT TUBA got the third most claps.

STEP ON NO PETS got the second most.

Janet's got the most. By far.

Ben had to admit, it deserved to.

"Janet and Kyle have pulled into the lead," said Mr. P.

Kyle gave Ben a look like a drumstick gives a drum.

"Time for the limericks!" said Mr. P. "I've been looking forward to this one." He looked at Ben as he said it. Mr. P. knew how much Ben loved limericks.

"Who wants to go first?"

Amy Lou Bonnerman raised her hand.

HEY FRIEND!

CALL ME FLYNN!

There was a horse with a hat.
I don't know what to say about that.
His name was Flynn.
I like him.
His friend was a bat.

It was *sort of* a limerick, thought Ben. But it lumbered along like a lopsided robot. Limericks were supposed to flow like music. And even though "Flynn" and "him" sounded similar, they didn't *exactly* rhyme, which bothered Ben, who preferred his rhymes to be *perfect*.

They went around
the room. Some of the
limericks were okay. Some
were barely acceptable. But
none of them were great.

Then it was Janet's turn:

There once was a person named Janet
Who came from an opposite planet.
Where fingers and toes
Grew out of your nose
And cotton balls were made of granite.

Ben liked Janet's limerick. It flowed like
music *and* it was funny.

He thought he could maybe write an even
better limerick, but . . . . he hadn't.

"Last up," said Mr. P., looking right at Ben. "I think we're in for a treat."

Ben felt sick to his stomach.

Throughout the week, he had written the first two lines of at least a dozen limericks. But he hadn't finished any of them because he had been waiting.

For what?

For someone else to write it? That didn't make any sense.

Ben loved writing. And he was good at it.

So what have I been waiting for? thought Ben. *Some things you just have to . . . do.*

It's your turn, Ben,

said Mr. P.

Ben looked around the room. Now everyone else was waiting for him. But he had nothing to show for all his patience.

The fortune had let him down. But that wasn't true, either.

228

The fortune was just a piece of paper.

He had let himself down.

He had let Walter down.

He had let Mr. P. down.

Ben was just about to give up, but then he remembered! He could make up limericks on the spot. He'd done it before. He was sure he could do it again.

There once was a . . .

But with everyone watching and waiting, it was impossible to reach into the part of his brain where the words were kept and the rhymes got made.

There once was a person . . .

Janet was giving him a *Come on, Ben, you can do it* kind of look.

Kyle was giving him a *You are about to lose this scavenger hunt* kind of look.

Walter was giving him a *Don't worry, Ben, everything is going to be okay* kind of look.

Walter was right. Everything was already okay. Ben loved writing limericks. That was what mattered. That was the fun part. Ben had nothing to prove.

"I'm sorry," said Ben. "Our team doesn't have one."

Janet shot Ben a *What the heck!* look. Ben not having a limerick was like a toothbrush not having bristles.

Mr. P. was also surprised. "Okay," he said, "in that case, the limerick winner is . . ."

"Actually," said Walter, "we *might* have one."

"We might?" said Ben.

"We *do*," said Walter, grinning like a cat with a plan.

"All right," said Mr. P. "Let's hear it."

Walter opened his notebook and began to read.

At first, no one said anything. Walter's limerick was really good, but no one was used to cheering for Walter, and they weren't sure how it worked.

"Ben" and "friend" don't rhyme!

said Kyle.

Ben was mad.

On one hand, Kyle was right. "Ben" and "friend" weren't perfect rhymes. But Walter had done something really good, and that was the important thing. In that moment, his rhymes were perfect *enough*.

Ben was just about to say so when Janet started talking instead.

"That was the greatest limerick I've ever heard!"

Ben wasn't sure that was true. Janet's limerick was probably better. Which made what she was doing all the more generous and wonderful.

Kyle scowled, but Janet ignored him like a ten-foot wave ignores a sandcastle.

"It was *definitely* better than mine," she said, giving Ben a look that was part wink and part high five.

Janet started to clap, and Ben clapped with her. Then Bob and Emma joined in. Then Kamari and Cole. Then, everyone but the pile of wet sand that was Kyle. Walter looked around in wide-eyed wonder. He beamed like someone who just put on his first pair of glasses and can suddenly see the pebbles on the sidewalk and the leaves on the trees.

"The judging is complete," said Mr. P. "You all did a great job, but Walter and Ben get the point!"

The class cheered again, especially Janet. The sound filled Ben's heart with joy, but his brain was too busy to hear it.

On one hand, the fortune had been wrong. Ben knew it was silly that he hadn't written a limerick.

But on the other hand, it had been right. If he had written a limerick, Walter wouldn't have had the chance to read his to the class.

And Walter reading his limerick to the class was a very good thing.

"That was amazing!" said Ben.

"You think so?" said Walter.

"The nicest limerick I've ever heard." It was absolutely true.

"You taught me how to do it!"

Ben smiled. He supposed he had.

"Do you know what this means?" Ben asked.

"We're definitely friends?"

Ben laughed.

"We are *definitely* friends. But it also means—"

"The score is tied again," said Mr. P., completing Ben's thought. "This is getting exciting."

Ben looked at Janet. Janet looked at Ben. Both of them smiled.

No matter what happened, everything was going to be okay.

CHAPTER 25

"Okay," said Mr. P. "Next question: Who knows Principal Hogan's middle name?"

Everyone looked at everyone else.

Ben knew that Kyle and Janet were going to get the point for the birthday question.

The only chance he and Walter had to tie in the overall standings was to break their promise to Principal Hogan.

But Ben wasn't going to do that. And he knew Walter wouldn't, either.

Everyone kept on saying nothing at all.

"So no one knows?" said Mr. P. Apparently, no one did.

"So, what is it?" asked Amy Lou Bonnerman.

I have no idea,

said Mr. P. with a disappointed sigh.

He refuses to tell me. I was really hoping one of you would figure it out.

Ben looked at Walter, and Walter looked at Ben. They shared a smile. It was wonderful and weird to have a secret that only the two of them knew. It might have been even better than earning the point.

"All right, then," said Mr. P. "Time for the final question. And since we have two teams with four points each, this one is the tiebreaker. Which three Honeycutt students have the same birthday?"

Ben closed his eyes. He was happy for Janet, but he couldn't bear to see the look on Kyle's face when they won.

He sat there waiting for Kyle or Janet to say the answer and get the point and win the scavenger hunt, but instead, all he heard was . . . nothing at all.

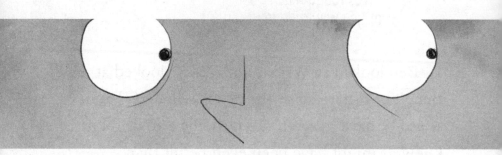

Ben opened his eyes and looked over at Kyle and Janet, who were looking over at Walter and him. Which meant . . .

They didn't have the answer, either!

Ben's mind went wild.

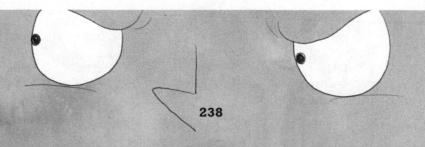

Between the four of them, they had asked every kid in school! Where had the Great Big Plan gone wrong? What had they missed? Ben couldn't figure it out.

"If no one has the answer, I guess we have a tie," said Mr. P.

Wait!

said Ben.

He felt like he was standing in the same room with the answer and was wearing a blindfold. All he had to do was fumble around in the dark until he found it. He just needed a little more time.

It was possible that a student was absent today. Or that someone had been in the nurse's office during lunch. Or that . . .

Ben realized their mistake.

They had forgotten about their own birthdays!

Ben had been in the October-through-December group, and his birthday was December 18. So if two other people shared his birthday, he would have found out.

Janet's birthday was March 24, so she had been with the right group, too.

Ben couldn't remember
Kyle's birthday, and Walter's . . . ?
Memories came into Ben's head like a
huge flock of birds all landing in the same
tree. He remembered being at one of
Walter's birthday parties. There had been a
corn maze. And gourds. It had been chilly.
In the fall. Probably November. He and
Walter had done a three-legged race called
the Turkey Trot because it had been
a few days before . . .

Ben's hand shot into the air.

I know the answer!

Yes, Ben?

The three students with the same birthday are Milo Acadio, Emmet Acadio, and . . .

Ben paused, wanting to

savor the moment . . .

Walter Stillman! They were all born on November twenty-first.

Correct!

said Mr. P.

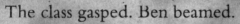

The class gasped. Ben beamed.

Walter burst into tears. The good kind.

CHAPTER 26

"We won!" said Ben. "Is that why you're crying? Because you're excited?"

"I'm glad we won," said Walter, "but that's not why I'm crying."

Then why?

Because you remembered my birthday.

Ben thought about the calendar and did some math. "Your birthday is this Sunday."

"Yes," said Walter. "I'm going to be nine."

Mr. P. paused, giving everyone a moment to enjoy the sheer anticipation. There was nothing as interesting and exciting as a prize in the moments before you find out what it is.

"To celebrate this week of thinking about words, I am delighted to bestow upon our winners a thesaurus and a rhyming dictionary."

Ben and Walter looked at each other with delight. They didn't need to discuss who would get which book. Walter picked up the thesaurus as if it held the secrets to every unsolved riddle. He opened to the first page and began to read.

Ben! Did you know that "ant bear" is a synonym for "aardvark"?

Ben didn't answer. He didn't even hear. He was lost in happiness as he read through the list of words that rhymed with "Ben."

Ten, when, pen, then, hen, yen, zen, again.

"Friend" wasn't on the list, of course, but as far as Ben was concerned, it would be from now on.

Through the haze of rhyming happiness, Ben heard Mr. P. say, "I'm sure this will come as a disappointment to everyone, but it's time for recess. I hear we're getting an extra half hour today."

Everyone cheered except Amy Lou Bonnerman.

"Multiplication drills," said Janet reassuringly.

Everyone put on their coats and lined up by the door.

"So," said Mr. P., coming over to Ben, "is there something I should know?"

"Nope," said Ben with a smile. "There is something you definitely *shouldn't* know."

Mr. P. gave a sly grin and left it at that as Ben ran off to enjoy the longest recess in the history of Honeycutt Elementary.

Ben saw Kyle and wondered if he'd be mad about not winning the scavenger hunt.

Kyle was not mad. Ben was relieved. Kyle was not perfect. But Kyle was his friend.

Come on, said Kyle.

Let's play snow-rules dodgeball.

Yes! said Ben.

In snow-rules dodgeball, you had to dodge regular balls *and* snowballs while also making sure no teachers saw you throwing snowballs, because throwing snowballs was not allowed. It was three kinds of dodging in one.

Ben couldn't wait. But first he had something to do.

"You go ahead," he said to Kyle. "I'll be there in a minute."

"Okay," said Kyle. He ran off with Lang.

Ben went to find Walter, who was reading his thesaurus on a snowy bench.

Great job, said Ben.

And so you know, you're the best partner I could have had.

What about Janet?

Janet was the best partner for Kyle. *You* were the best partner for me.

Do you mean it?

I do.

They sat there for a few seconds just feeling good.

"My birthday party is on Sunday. Want to come?" Walter was looking down like he was expecting Ben to say no.

"Yes," said Ben. "Of course!"

Walter lit up like a sparkler at night.

"I can only invite three people," said Walter. It was a very specific number.

"Who all is coming so far?"

"You."

"What kind of party is it?"

"It's a surprise," said Walter. "I think you'll like it, though."

"I'm sure I will," said Ben.

Ben remembered. He was supposed to go sledding with Janet on Sunday.

"Could Janet come, too?"

"Sure!" said Walter. "If you think she'd want to."

"I bet she would," said Ben. Janet was always game for whatever. It was one of the things Ben liked best about her.

Janet would make it even more fun. Two people was just two people. Three people was a group of friends.

CHAPTER 27

Ben was right. Janet did want to go to Walter's party. Ben's dad drove them to the address Walter had written down for Ben. It was way out in the countryside.

"Where are we?" Janet asked as they drove through acres of wide-open fields.

"No idea," said Ben.

Ben's dad just smiled. Sometimes it was more fun not to know where you were headed.

After they'd been driving for a while, Janet pulled something out of her pocket and handed it to Ben.

It was a letter addressed to Janet from a Dot Babcock.

"Is this—?"

"Yes," said Janet. Her face was calm.

"But what—?"

"It arrived a few months ago, but my mom forgot to give it to me. We were talking about Dot last night and she remembered."

"Can I—?"

"Yes," said Janet. "I think you should."

Ben could hardly contain his anticipation as he unfolded the letter. He would finally find out what had actually happened between Janet and Dot. He would finally know how to keep it from happening to him.

Dear Janet,

I got your letter. Sorry I hurt your feelings. I wish I could take it all back. I don't know why I acted like that.

Tiffany and I aren't friends anymore. She said I was boring. Now she's friends with Jackqi. Remember when we braided our hair together for a day? And when we painted those rocks with secret messages and left them in people's yards? I miss doing things like that. I wish you still lived here. I hope you found a new best friend as great as you are.

Love
DOT

p.s. Tiffany's chinchilla bit her in the nose.

Ben didn't know what to say. His heart was churning and his mind was racing. Even Dot didn't have the answers. Whatever had gone wrong was still a mystery.

Ben was tired of waiting to find out. He needed to *do* something.

Promise me that—

I can't, said Janet, putting her hand on Ben's hand and giving him a look so serious that he swallowed the rest of his sentence.

I can't promise *anything.*

Why not?

Ben was devastated.

Because that's not how it actually works.

It's not?

"I don't think so. Dot promised to be my friend forever, and look what happened. Promises don't actually mean anything. But if you and I agree to treat each other kindly and always tell each other the truth, I'm pretty sure the rest will take care of itself."

It wasn't the certainty that Ben had been hoping for, but he had the sense that it was as close as he was going to get.

"I'll do my best," he said.

"Me too," said Janet.

"You promise?"

Janet laughed.

Yes. That part I can promise.

Ben held out his hand to shake on it.

But Janet leaned over and gave him a great
big hug instead. She seemed to have
forgotten that they were not the kind
of friends who hugged.

Ben saw his dad give a
smile in the rearview mirror.

What the heck?

thought Ben.
He hugged back.

253

After a while,
they parked by a big
red barn. Walter was
there with his mom
and a baby.

"Hi, Ben," said Walter's mom. It had been a
long time since he'd seen her.

"Hi," he said. "This is Janet."

Walter's mom gave Janet a huge smile.
"Walter says you're very smart," she said.

"It's true!" said Walter.

"Thanks," said Janet, blushing a little.

"Who's this?" Ben's dad asked,
tickling the baby's chin.

"This is Ajax," said
Walter's mom.

WHAT?!

"I forgot to tell you," said Walter. "We stole your great idea."

"Careful," said Ben's dad to Walter's mom. "Ben might ask you to adopt him."

Ben was staring at the baby. He couldn't understand how something so tiny could also be a human being.

"Do you want to hold him?" asked Walter's mom.

Part of Ben wanted to and part of him didn't, but the wanting part won out. Ben nodded.

Walter's mom showed Ben how to hold his arms like a cradle and then handed him the baby. Ajax blinked at Ben and reached his tiny fingers toward Ben's face.

It was like holding a piece of someone's heart. The baby was light as a bird. And incredibly soft. And extremely *smelly*.

Ben suddenly realized how Walter had come up with the baby fart answer.

He gave the baby back.

"Thanks," he said.

"He likes you," said Walter's mom.

Ben smiled. The day kept getting better.

"Come on!" said Walter. He led Ben and Janet around the barn. A man was standing by an enormous basket attached to a gigantic piece of red cloth that spread like spilled paint across the field.

Surprise! said Walter.

Oh yes! said Janet.

I've always wanted to do this.

What is it? Ben asked.

"You're going
to love it!" she said. The
man lit a flame and held up one
end of the cloth. Ben realized that the
ocean of red was actually an enormous
bag. Slowly it started to fill with hot air.
It grew fuller and fuller, and Ben understood.
It was an enormous balloon. Eventually,
it lifted into the air and tugged
against ropes that were
holding the basket
in place.

Time to get in,

said the man.

Ben wasn't sure. He was suddenly a big fan of
the ground.

"Come on," said Janet, getting in. "This is going to be great."

Ben got in. Janet made it feel okay. Walter got in, too.

"Ready?" said the man.

"Ready," said Walter.

"Ready," said Janet.

Ben was not ready. He thought about telling Janet and Walter to go on without him. But instead, he waited just long enough that it was too late to back out. Suddenly the basket rose into the air. Ben didn't want to look down. He felt strange tingles in his stomach and toes.

"Happy birthday, Walter!" said Janet.

"This is the best birthday ever!" said Walter.

Ben clutched the side of the basket and shut his eyes tight.

"It's beautiful, beautiful. It's beautiful, Ben." Janet held Ben's hand and squeezed it tight. "Open your eyes, silly."

Ben did. There were Janet and Walter with the biggest smiles.

"Look," said Walter, pointing.

Ben looked.

The world was like a model, like a
map. Like an endless kingdom filled
with all of the wonderful things they had
not yet done together.

They raced along, lifting higher and
higher. There was no question. Ben was
flying. He had been waiting his whole
life to feel this way.

Flying with his friends. In the
sky. On a beautiful, beautiful day.
Into the endless and unknowable future.
It was worth every bit of waiting that had
led to this moment.

It was a good thing. A very good thing.
The very best thing of all.

ABOUT THE AUTHOR AND ILLUSTRATOR

Hello, friends! My name is Matthew, and I wrote this book.

And I'm Robbi. I drew the pictures.

ALDEN

KATO

AUGUST

JASPER

Matthew: And, well . . . ?

Robbi: What *else* should we tell them?

M: Well, we *could* tell them that we're married and have four kids.

R: Good idea! And maybe we should mention that we live in an old barn in Maryland, where we've been making books together for the past fifteen years.

M: Yep, that's all good stuff, but . . . there is so much room left on this page. Our readers demand inspiring content!

We could dance?

Good idea!

I just heard one reader cringe and another one yawn.

We need to try *harder*.

I agree. You first.

M: Are you trying to scare our readers away?

R: No way. I'm trying to inspire them.

M: I think it's working! *Keep going!*

R: Every summer, I travel to an off-the-grid corner of the Alaskan tundra and pull salmon from the Bering Sea using my bare hands and muscly thumbs. While wearing rubber pants.

M: Weirdly, all of this is true.

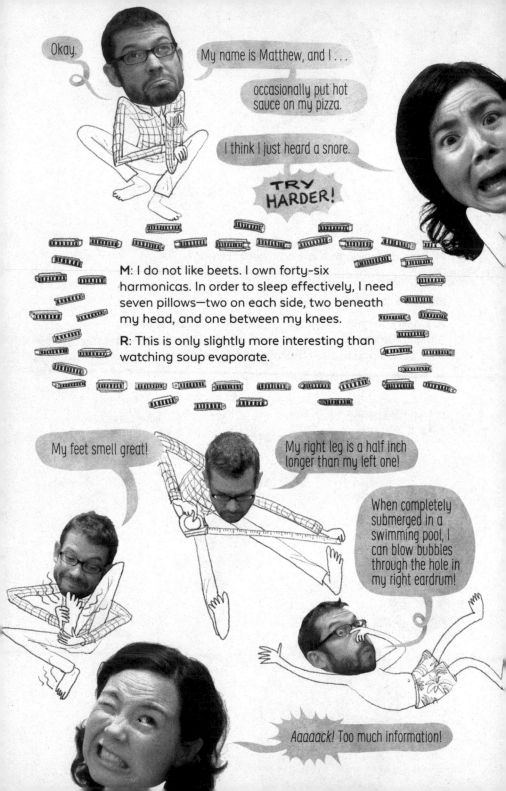

M: That was fun. I feel better now.

R: Our readers are no longer inspired. Now they are worried. I hope you're finished.

M: Nope. I'm also going to tell them how to contact us.

R: So they can learn more about your ears and feet?

Yes. *And* so they can . . .

- Join our mailing list
- Write us a note
- Ask us to speak at a school, library, or conference

You brave souls can find us at

robbiandmatthew.com

OR find us on
YouTube: Robbi & Matthew and
Instagram: Robbi.and.Matthew

We promise there will be no more dancing.

I make no such promises.

GOOD THINGS YOU (REALLY DO) HAVE TO WAIT FOR

Waiting is not such a great idea when it comes to doing your chores, apologizing to your friends, or writing a haiku, but there are some good things that you definitely do have to wait for.

For example, it takes about eight to twelve whole minutes for chocolate chip cookies to bake, and then you have to wait even longer before taking a bite if you don't want to burn the roof of your mouth.

And if you want to have a glass of extremely cold lemonade with your

cookies, you'll have to wait three to four hours for the water in your freezer to turn into ice cubes.

Perhaps you enjoy gazing at wildlife while eating your snack? Keep in mind that it will take weeks or even months for the caterpillar in that chrysalis to turn into a butterfly. (I hope you baked a lot of cookies.)

Maybe, like Ben, you are waiting for a little brother or sister. Keep in mind that human babies take approximately nine months to grow and develop before they're born. If that seems like too long to wait, just be glad you're not an elephant. Their babies gestate for up to twenty-two months!

ANY DAY NOW WOULD BE FINE...

19, 20, 21, 22...

Your birthday (hooray!) happens for just twenty-four hours out of the 8,760 hours in a year, which means that you spend 99.73 percent of your life waiting for your birthday and just 0.27 percent actually enjoying it. And that's only if you stay up for all twenty-four hours of each birthday. (Note: We definitely do not recommend this.)

.27%

99.73%

☐ YOUR BIRTHDAY
■ THE REST OF THE YEAR

I'M FINALLY TWO!

Unless . . . your birthday is on leap day, which happens only once every four years!

I'M STILL ZERO!

If you are waiting to *start* losing your baby teeth, it usually happens around age six. If you are waiting to *stop* losing your baby teeth, *that* usually happens around age twelve. If you are hoping not to lose any more teeth after that, try daily flossing and not playing ice hockey.

HEY!!

If you really want to test your patience, look up at the sky and wait for Halley's Comet, a massive hunk of ice, rock, dust, and gases that shows up once every seventy-five years. The good news: You can see it from Earth! The bad news: It won't be back until 2061.

The next Cookie Chronicles book (*Ben Yokoyama and the Cookie of Perfection*) is scheduled to be published in December 2021. Which means that, depending on what date it is now, you either have to wait a really long time or only as long as it takes to get to the library.

WOOT!

CONCLUSION:
Be glad you're not a cookie-eating, comet-watching, butterfly-loving, little-brother-wanting elephant that was born on leap day.

Also, floss your teeth.

Join Ben on his latest adventure!

CHAPTER 2

Ben liked school. He liked to learn. He liked seeing his friends. And he liked playing kickball at recess.

But as he stood there waiting for the bell, he didn't have the heart to listen as Kyle and Lang argued over who could kick the kickball highest. He didn't have the patience to ask what new huge words Walter had learned or to say nice things about Darby's latest gymnastics trick.

What's *wrong* with you?

asked Janet impatiently.

Ben wasn't sure what to say. His mad had turned to sad. Sad was for sitting down, so he sat on a bench and sighed again, daydreaming that a careless millionaire might wander by and drop a gold nugget at his feet.

Janet shook her head and walked over to chat with Kamari, who was chatting with Darrow and Beckett. Ben sat and sighed and glanced around. Everyone else was smiling and laughing like it was the greatest day in history, which made Ben all the more miserable and hopeless. He needed comfort. He needed

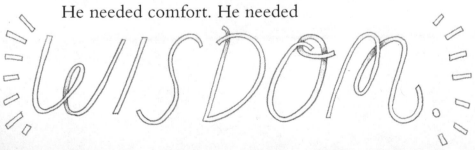

WISDOM.

Then it hit Ben: he knew an
easy way to get both!
He opened his backpack
and found his lunch bag. He
undid the latch, reached
inside, and pulled out
his fortune cookie.

It caught the attention of Janet, who marched
over with the anxious expression of someone
about to witness a terrible accident. "What's
going on here, Ben?"

He ignored her and started to remove the
clear plastic wrapper from the cookie. A tiny part
of his brain knew he was making a mistake.

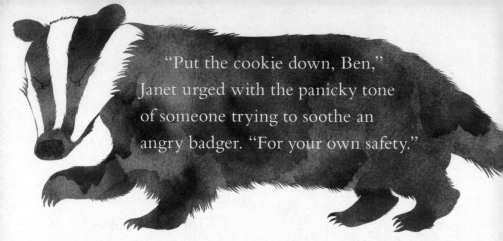

"Put the cookie down, Ben," Janet urged with the panicky tone of someone trying to soothe an angry badger. "For your own safety."

Ben had a vague sense that she was right, but it was already too late. He had unleashed a chain of events with such force and momentum that not even a Janet could stop them.

Ben held the cookie up to his nose and took a deep sniff.

"Think of the consequences, Ben!"

But consequences were something that happened *later*. Ben was more concerned with right *now*.

He closed his eyes and savored the immediate future.

Ben anticipated the satisfying crack as the cookie broke open. The flood of flavor as he popped it in his mouth. The thrilling surge of wisdom as he read the fortune it contained. The cookie would know how to make him feel better. It always did.

Ben felt a whoosh as soft as a whisper.

W H O O O O O O O S H

Suddenly the weight of the cookie
disappeared from his hands, as if it had been
lifted by the wind or stolen by an angel.

Ben opened his eyes and immediately wanted
to close them again.

What he saw was not okay.

CHAPTER 3

First Ben saw the feet
and then the teeth.
And then he felt the
menacing glare.
His cookie was
gone. The questions
were why, how, and
who? The answers
were perfectly clear.
Flegg was standing
there, holding Ben's
cookie. Flegg
McEggers. Tall,
strong, and
terrifying.

Flegg was in
fifth grade, outweighed
Ben two to one, and was
approximately eighteen inches
taller. Everyone was afraid of
Flegg. Because Flegg
was the *worst*.

Ben even had a special set of Flegg-related rules:

#1

Always know exactly where Flegg is

and

#2

Always keep tasty treats hidden from view.

Now Ben had made the double mistake of closing his eyes *and* flaunting his cookie.

The only person who wasn't afraid of Flegg was Janet.

Whatcha doing there, big guy?

she asked, waving her
arms to get his attention.

**How about giving
Ben's cookie back?**

Janet was trying to sound casual and cool, but
Ben knew it wouldn't work.

"Why?" Flegg seemed genuinely confused, as
if Janet were suggesting he shave off one of his
eyebrows. "It's in *my* hand now."

"Right, but it belongs to Ben," Janet explained,
a little worked up, but not yet
hopping mad.

Ben's heart
pounded and his
stomach clenched.
He felt sick and
scared and ashamed.

He wished *he* were
the one standing up to Flegg
instead of sitting there wilting
like an unwatered plant . . .
but Janet was so much
better at it.

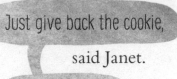

Just give back the cookie, said Janet.

It isn't yours.

But I want to eat it, Flegg reasoned.

GIVE. IT. BACK!

shouted Janet, lunging for the cookie like a chipmunk lunges at a grizzly bear. But Flegg held the cookie high above his head, where Janet couldn't reach it.

"What *is* it, anyway?" Flegg asked, examining the cookie carefully.

"It's just a cookie. It's not even that tasty," Janet insisted.

Flegg held the cookie right in front of his face. "It doesn't *look* like a cookie. But it *smells* like one."

Flegg opened his mouth. Ben saw what was about to happen. He had to act now, or all would be lost.

"Wait!" he shouted. "You can't just *eat* it. There's a piece of *paper* inside."

Stop trying to trick me.

Flegg scowled.

I'm not stupid.

Flegg looked down at Ben like a tower looks down at its shadow.

"Ben's telling the truth!" said Janet, holding up her hands to show she meant no harm. "I know it sounds strange, but inside that cookie is a tiny strip of paper that gives you advice."

"That is the weirdest thing I've ever heard." Flegg seemed ever-so-slightly curious.

"You're not wrong," Janet admitted. "But . . . here's the thing . . ."

Ben could see the sprig of an idea sprouting in her magnificent mind.

> Whatever the fortune says *comes true*! For example, that one might say "Stealing is wrong, so give Ben his cookie or else you'll get hit by an asteroid."

> It doesn't say that,

said Flegg in a way that seemed ever-so-slightly concerned.

"But it *could*," Janet insisted. "Who do you think would win in a fight between you and an asteroid, Flegg?"

Ben wasn't sure the answer was clear.

"Or . . . ," Janet continued. "What if it says 'People wearing purple pants will get eaten by a tiger today'?"

Ben hadn't noticed, but Flegg's pants were purple.

How does the cookie know what color my pants are?

Flegg asked, his eyes wide.

"The cookie knows *everything*," said Janet in a sinister whisper, as if sharing a delicious secret. "It peeks into your soul and gives you *exactly* the advice you need."

You're not
making sense,

said Flegg.

I never follow
advice.

Ben believed it.

"It sounds to me like maybe you're not
really interested in the fortune?" Janet prompted.

"Not really," said Flegg, as if they were
discussing an extremely rotten egg.

"That's great," said Janet. "How about *you*
keep the cookie and *Ben* takes that pesky fortune
off your hands?"

Flegg's scowl relaxed as he considered his
options. For just a moment, a door opened inside
him, maybe wide enough to sneak a cookie
through.

What do you say, Ben?

Janet asked, nodding vigorously
to steer Ben toward the right
answer.

Don't you think you can *share* with Flegg?

Ben was torn. He glanced around. Everyone
was watching. Everyone was waiting to see
what he would do next. Ben appreciated
that Janet was trying to help him, but
it wasn't okay for Flegg to keep
pushing him around.
He needed to prove
it to everyone.
And to himself.

"I'd . . . prefer to have the fortune *and* the cookie, if you don't mind."

Flegg looked wounded. His open door slammed shut, and the brutal expression returned. "That's not very generous of you."

"It really isn't," hissed Janet, shooting Ben a blistering scowl. "I'm doing my best here, Ben!"

Actually, I want both things,

Flegg declared, suddenly realizing he had absolutely no reason to compromise.

If I have to, I can take my purple pants off.

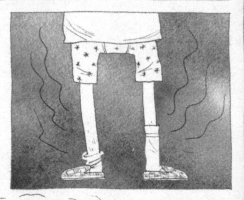

Ben watched with HORROR as Flegg broke the cookie open.

Look, there's a piece of paper inside!

Flegg announced gleefully.

Yes, that's the fortune,

said Janet with exasperation.

That's what we've been talking about.

It's so tiny!

Flegg was extremely pleased.

Tiny and *dangerous*,

Janet reminded him.

This is your last chance to save yourself by giving it to Ben. Then you can eat your cookie and be on your way.

I'm going to tear it up. That way the asteroid can't get me.

WAIT! said Ben, jolted from his petrified stupor.

First just tell me what it says.

The fortune was a shred of precious wisdom. Ben couldn't live with the thought of never knowing what it said.

Ben's desperate tone must have touched some speck of humanity deep within the heart of Flegg. He blinked at Ben and then squinted down at the fortune.

"It says . . ."

The best things in life are free.

It took a moment for the wisdom to claw its way from Flegg's lips to Ben's embattled brain, but once it landed, Ben's sadness zoomed away like spring arriving on a sudden breeze and vanquishing the darkest winter.

All his problems were solved!

The Astrostar was the *best* scooter. And now it was *free*!

Mama Mia's almond kisses were the *best* treat! And now he could have as many as he liked *without paying a penny*!

Ben didn't need the cookie itself. With this fortune, he'd get everything he'd ever wanted.

I'll share!

he said, leaping to his feet.

You can keep the cookie, Flegg. I'll take the fortune!

No way. Flegg frowned.

I like it. It's *mine.*

He popped the cookie into his mouth with one hand and shoved the fortune deep into his pocket with the other. "Mmmm," he said. "That's *goooooood.*"

He smiled a smile that hit Ben like a bazooka blast, then turned and walked away with great booming strides toward another group of kids who weren't paying quite enough attention.

"And *stay* out!" Janet yelled. It was what Bigger Llama always said when she'd managed to chase the pesky emus out of the roller rink in their favorite show, *Snooptown.*

But Flegg didn't even look back. As he
Flegged his way across the grass, kids scattered
like there was a force field around him.

Which, in a way, there was.

Flegg was Flegg. He always had been. He
always would be. And there was absolutely
nothing you could do about it.

THE COOKIE CHRONICLES

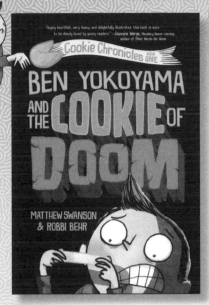

"Hugely heartfelt, very funny, and delightfully illustrated, this book is sure to be deeply loved by young readers." —Jasmine Warga, Newbery Honor–winning author of Other Words for Home

Cookie Chronicles BOOK ONE

BEN YOKOYAMA AND THE COOKIE OF DOOM

MATTHEW SWANSON & ROBBI BEHR

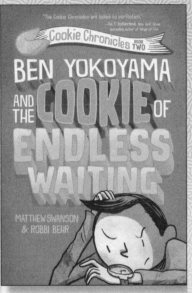

"The Cookie Chronicles are baked to perfection." —Tui T. Sutherland, New York Times bestselling author of Wings of Fire

Cookie Chronicles BOOK TWO

BEN YOKOYAMA AND THE COOKIE OF ENDLESS WAITING

MATTHEW SWANSON & ROBBI BEHR

"Great characters, hilarious jokes, and delightful drawings make each page a joy to read." —Lincoln Peirce, New York Times bestselling author of Big Nate

Cookie Chronicles BOOK THREE

BEN YOKOYAMA AND THE COOKIE OF PERFECTION

MATTHEW SWANSON & ROBBI BEHR

"The Cookie Chronicles are baked to perfection." —Tui T. Sutherland, New York Times bestselling author of Wings of Fire

Cookie Chronicles BOOK FOUR

BEN YOKOYAMA AND THE COOKIE THIEF

MATTHEW SWANSON & ROBBI BEHR

DON'T MISS A SINGLE BITE!